Unconditional Secrets Beyond Love

Written by Marlies van den Broek compiled by Marlies. Unconditional Secrets Beyond Love is a rebranded love story. The best released in 2024-century. The best of the early twenties and before with over 10 years of being unpublished until this publication in the 20s century. Now that it has been published and shared it has been passionately rebranded and compiled with the writing by really beautiful people in helping her and find sources to her manuscript. Special thanks to all who helped. She loved to know that fabulous people loved reading "Beyond Unconditional Love" that belongs to this edition of fantasy romance and for readers to mention the parts they enjoy reading.

Unconditional Secrets Beyond Love

A story from the heart for a heart

By Marlies van den Broek

© 2025 Marlies van den Broek
Publisher: BoD · Books on Demand GmbH,
In de Tarpen 42, 22848 Norderstedt, bod@bod.de
Print: Libri Plureos GmbH, Friedensallee 273,
22763 Hamburg
ISBN: 978-3-7693-1967-5

By Marlies van den Broek

Unconditional Secrets Beyond Love

The start of a growth full romance. The daughter and son of thunder, lightning, beauty and the moon and more, half human half wolf – the Halflings are on trip by the poisonous of love of their adventures through hell, Dorthrin and beyond. Enjoying the life in the civilized world that their parent L and S left behind in a heritage. They meet joyful, cozy, crazy, generous and gorgeous new demonic friends and enemies shall always lure, stuck between two worlds, might even fall head-over-heels leaving you with the curiosity of the secrets of lovemaking. It was the perfect flight.

Part 1

The Halflings had names that
consisted of more than 1 letter. The
boy was named Raphael and was
the healer of kids that were hurt by
demons. The girl was named Uriela
and brought the children into light
towards the purgatory world. Both
last 2 letters were created in the
deepest fires of hell, el. The twins
carried protection and were the most
powerful beasts in both worlds, the
civilized world and hell. Bringing
protection of justice, mercy and
righteousness. Their zodiac sign
were sagittarius and lion. But twins.
The twins were messengers of their
parents. They could predict the birth
of innocent souls and the death of
demonic vampires, pedophiles and
evil citizens. With black roses in her
hands, Uriela, she stood famous as a
virgin in hell like Maria in heaven.
Both had the power to come across

dangerous flashes and to gear them. They became the guardians of modern technology like the radio, television and *smartphones*. Both had discipline with the energy weapon of wisdom from their parents. Both created harmony on earth and an agreement in hell with their cleanses of beauty. Just like their stunning appearances. Both lend a hand to the lost souls to find a path in their lives on earth and in hell. They protected children once they were born to be to the fore of their enemies, demonic souls, by teaching them and handing them a knife to strike into pedophiles cross at a young age.

Raphael was the curer who came out first out of L her placenta. Healer of travelers. Showing the right way through hell. With his passion for healing innocent souls of children of lions and sagittarius just like his parents. He wasn't born only for the cure of children that became victim of demons, but he actually also healed lives of beasts, shrubberies and creatures from the darkest flames of hell. He was a lion and she was a sagittarius but both born at the same time out of the placenta from their mother.

Uriela, she was the twin of fire, flames and light. With a burning sward she was a timepiece ruling over thunder and terror. She could predict this. As a leader of the gates of hell she warned the lives in Dorthrin against danger from hell. She was the shield and watcher over the deathful temple of lost souls. She is the flame of hell. She became the twin of study, school, exams, writing and an alchemist.

Both were seen as the twins of creating music. She was still a virgin

until she met him. The lost soul of
the flight plane.

All shimmering imprints from L and
S their death, with the shimmering
lights on sunrises and sunsets. The
shimmering imprints the twins had
was to make their parents rise from
their death. Walking on undefined
roads. The twins where born while
both parents were still alive before
their death. They grew up as angel
twins but devilish and didn't mind
that their parents weren't alive. They
were distracted by ecstasy from the
life in Dorthrin. The beasts, creatures
and shrubberies nursed them every
single day to become courageous,
well-mannered twins. Such bravery
in those children who grew up.
After the death of their parents the
twins reached out to them by
writing letters and replies to the
letters their parents left behind
before her death.

The mother of the twins lived alone in a small village in Droplet Cloud, She had one brother and two sisters that had lived. L, she was close to them and all had a special bond. A joyful and magical bond with a life growing together before parting. Their mother met his man of his dreams, their future father in an unconditional magical way. But both didn't last long in Dorthrin or the civilized world once they, L and S as parents said "yes" to be together for eternity in those worlds. Their mother, L, dies first followed by a suicide execution of their father.

The father of the twins lived among beasts, shrubberies and creatures in the mountains and in Dorthrin in a small village, *Superbia*. Nearby the waters of the sea. He had a sister and no brother and was the only emperor wolf of the family. He had a strong bond with her. He was exceptionally rich and lived a rich life. He dressed in expensive clothing's, if possible, he would get his own haute couture. When both parents lived, they had a remarkably rich life with their children when they were babies only. They owned many luxury houses and had stacks of money. Left for the twins to use a richer life. S, in his youth he had many beastly, creaturely and shrubbery friends he grew up with. S and L their meeting was planned and from the moment they met in their later years it was love at first sight. The train. They got married after some time. It was a December night when L was still human and gave birth to twins, their Halflings Raphael and Uriela.

All imprints shall fade away. Once the twins finish their highest degree of school one of their beloved shrubberies died on earth to relive in

Dorthrin. It was a gloominess hyacinth with all its beauty and smell that resulted in a blooming flower in Dorthrin with the power to release a smell to mislead the servants of Satan to make them pass Superbia to hunt on innocent flowers elsewhere to drawn the shrubberies, creatures and beasts into the deepest fires of hell.

The twins decided to build an own business after finishing their university, a bar with liquor and drugs on the beaches nearby the sea. They avoided entering a duty in the military service of Dorthrin and earth once they turned 18. It was a matter of time for formation. At school in Dorthrin the beasts, shrubberies and creatures thought the twins Latin and Satan's language that was a Latin dialect besides Swahili to communicate with the life in Dorthrin. Whoever learnt Satin's dialect had the power to become an emperor in the deepest fires of hell, hell itself. The business near the sea was a booming business for humans in the civilized world and for changelings, transformed lives from Dorthrin. Both twins met there their friends. Enlightened souls from the sea. Once met, they decided to challenge their ability to fly. The twins would never give birth or get in an engagement with their ghost friends. It's a list. While studying for a specialism in the civilized world and Dorthrin they yearned for their parents letters that they received to read once passing for an exam. Hoping to find a *á la recherché du temps* to reveal their deaths mystery. They craved for the shimmering dream to touch their imprints. With sunrise and sunset.

Death fades everything and calls for souls to be taken from a life that once lived. After the death of their parents, the twins couldn't let go of their death. They both felt miserable for a long time that they had other thoughts with their ruling powers and abilities. They had mysterious, magical and mad thoughts. That, while being raised in worlds with good intentions.

It was spring day that their father and mother left them to be nursed by their family and relatives in Dorthrin. Their body was a mystery. No grave and no place to remember their parents. Letters only. Once the news hit Dorthrin about L and S, the beasts, creatures and shrubberies in Dorthrin cried a sadly melody. It was an unattainable death. Impossible. They felt empty, the twins cried everywhere they traveled. Until in their later ages they could exchange a few words and commune with their parents and found and read more letters that L left for them. The formation would be their ticket to end their sorrows and their parents shall always remain in their history.

Being children of the richest parents they start forgetting after partying with many drugs. Losing expensive jewels and forgetting to remember where they left their most expensive precious bits and pieces. Assuming that a demon stole their objects but were actually lost in the fires of hell. Even accusing some demons for taking their belongings. They became lost. It's hard to remember under influence of cocaine and MDMA-crystals. What was lost had consequences of whose death would follow. All shimmering imprints shall disappear.

There were plenty of times to yearn for preciousness. A lost diamond on a ring, or misplaced pumps. The golden time. Owning gold isn't something magical in Dorthrin. In the civilized world owning golden time is being admired. The magic and mystery of the wonderers of the golden time didn't lose touch while being admired by humans, some demonic. Although the time of gold was gifted, once gliding a watch around your wrist it states something indefinable.

A power-breakage. A champagne bottle popped open at the bar and two glasses of champagne were filled. "All ours now"

"Just the way we wanted"

The stars in the galaxy are getting clearer.

The lost souls in the sea cry.

They are more than siblings. Their unconditional love for each other started to grow during their adventures in between worlds. Both often talked about him and her with their shrubbery friends, creaturely friends and beasty friends in the company of wolves pack.

One thing she is, isn't sexy. What she is? She is clumsy!

One moment they ran into each other using cocaine. Both had a few lines and liquor drinks. At last it seemed to be happening! They flirted! On the dance floor they moved towards each other. They explored each other's bodies on the dance floor. They looked at each other. Finally it happened. The first kiss!

The first kiss. Didn't go exactly as it was supposed to be. She bumped her nose on his ghostly chin. It happened at the moment when they were about to kiss each other. Sexy? Not really. Funny? Yes. And they burst out laughing out of clumsiness. He grabbed her and hugged her and kissed her forehead. The moment of romance was gone.

Later that night she received a *Whatsapp* message from her ghost friend.

"We still have to finish something, are you coming home with me?"

She searched for him in the crowd and together they drove to his house. He didn't give her the chance to close the door and he grabbed her head and their lips met. A magic spark tingled tickling her entire body.

He took of his shoes and lifted her up on his way to the bedroom and he accidently bumped his toe against the corner of the bed.

"Ouch!" he yelled. "I think we're both clumsy" "I think so too," she laughed.

"Show me where it hurts, should I kiss it?" He grabbed her loose hair and held it tightly together. He gave her control while he kissed her open wound and sucked the blood out of it.

He pulled off his shirt. His skin glittered of sweat. She masturbated him with both hands. As she did him, she pulled of her top and he grabbed her breasts. "Can I" as he lifted her up.

As she stood up. His hands slid to open her bra. She pulled off her skirt and shoes. "Wow" he screamed surprisingly. And she lay herself down on the bed. "Can I" he asked. As she opened her legs and nodded. He crawled demonically between her legs as he used his mouth to pull her thong down her legs.

Then she felt his tongue in a slow, soft stroke over her sensitive spot. Moving slowly, moving consciously, moving sexy! She got hotter and wetter! She grabbed his head firmly and pushed him deeper between her legs. He now made small, fast circles, around her most sensitive spot.

In the meantime he slowly slid 1 finger inside her. She threw her hands loose to grab the bed. She accidently knocked a glass of liquor on the floor that fell with a loud bang, spoiling a piece of the cocaine that lay rested on the glass table.

"Shit" she shouted

"Cunt, sorry" he replied

"This isn't really going well, is it," she laughed

"I actually think you're doing really well" she winked

"Do you want me to take you now then?" he whispered

She replies with a bite in her lips.

He lifted her and put her down in doggy. He pushed himself inside her and grabbed her hands behind her. With her face in the mattress to push himself hard and deep inside her. They both moaned loudly of pleasure. Not long after he lays himself down next to her moaning. Both came. She got out of bed and when she returned to the living he prepared some cocaine and they made love repeatedly. It lasted all night long.

"My beauty"

It felt good. For some past time after having followed him, a marvelous friend, all the things started to come closely and she writes a captivated letter to her mother, wherever she may be. In her bed she thought of her and wished she would be here to love her darkened soul and see her growth, she and her brother became almost full grown now. She couldn't feel her imprint anymore and sometimes she did. It was only if

something good was coming on
their path in flanking by worlds that
a slight imprint would occur.
Halfling Uriela, she rises now in hell
alongside with her brother, Raphael,
and both decided to travel
sometimes to other villages outside
Dorthrin Firegale, hanging around
demonic streets, both seeking
demonic souls, devilish and divines
even the ones who would truest
commit a sin to obey their souls. At
night the Halflings looked at their
demonic friendly ghost entities that
they became friends with, with
terrified eyes. They told the twins
that they were looking for a friend,
two friendly souls, without telling
their clandestine competed in hell,
that they did find the one and truest
deal in them.

The Halfling's love was patience and
kind. Their love didn't create
jealousy. The Halflings felt the need

to be imperative and kind towards demons and immortals ruling each kingdom of hell. They never told their ghostly friends, who grew their powers when kissing which was known in hell as a surreptitious towards the Halflings, when the Halflings would get back from their rendezvous from the civilized world, hell and Dortrhin. Uriela and Raphael regularly asked their ghostly friends to kiss them because their curse from hell was a kiss fatale. Their ghost friends kiss. Their kisses were incomparably beyond the Halflings feelings of thrill, and that under the galaxy of stars on planet earth at the seas beach. As if the love grew sturdy. The Halflings believed that four is better than two, because it is a good reward for a short-term power in hell. The Halflings and their demonic friends were inseparable for many years after their change. Demons now lift them up with the gathered souls from the Sea and other continental gates in the civilized world and villages in hell, some similar to Superbia. There is enough to feed in towns where spirits sin on greed, wrath, envy, lust, gluttony and sloth.

The Halflings had many sex on earth and in hell with their demonic new friends. A clandestine kept away from Dorthrin but was very much known and wasn't a surprise in hell among the eyes of Satan pledged to the daughter of S and L. Raphael, laid his other sex, his exotic ghostly skeleton love, gently down in bed and roughly took his clothes off. He played with toys. As a surprise of how experienced he was. He really left the lovers in bed with their eyes burning in higher flames. After she climaxed several times he penetrated her deeply. She was extremely wet. There was no time for room service in hell with an excellent iced champagne with strawberries or *Las Puerta's – Cabernet Sauvignon* from Acid Chile, instead she would admit that he broke her skeleton that he would heal her with his malevolent powers of flaming wind blowing circles on her nipples and belly. He would gently turn her around and make her come even more than 50 times.

The Halflings when they are together with their lovers, they keep it warm, they love their demonic skeleton lovers, and let them follow their dreams. They couldn't bring them to their family's place. Both spoke in the language of *Satan*, without having to speak Latin. They have the love. Both are clumsy. If they only had the power of the mysteries of their devilish soul and knowledge to feed on sinners' souls, so as to move mountains like their lovers do with their fatal kiss. In hell, they didn't have love and without love they just couldn't speak. The Halflings and their demonic ghostly skeleton friends filled each other up with highly gifted language. They spoke. They spoke in the language of music that the Halflings were gifted with by their parents and was understood by their malevolent ghostly entities. The love they had geared all things and endured everything. For some passing time the Halflings wrote a letter to their grandfather *Lucifer* and grandmother *Medusa* to bring out the overwhelming news to their raising parents that the Halflings will marry their fading ghostly friends and sent them a one-way ticket to the Sea for this one-day event. Lucifer and Medusa didn't trust this event that much and alleged it was just another bet from a chess game played by the twins to amuse themselves.

Wondering where their children are and questioning herself if they ever met her along the way in the clouds, are they currently on an adventure with friends or does *Satan* have a better plan on how they will live their young life? She hopes to meet her twins one day, maybe 9 years from now. She can decipher the thought of her children being in a commitment to succeed in life. She is ready. S is worried for their children to come across the lands of *Invidia*. Soon enough this won't matter because S has a better plan. L and S want to meet their children so badly, the Halflings. They will go on adventures together. Together like ice put beside a raging fire! The twins are probably in love before they will meet their mother L and father S in an ambiguous mystical appearance in the mountains. They would probably see signs of *Jesus Christ his mother Maria* but that's okay, no matter how long it takes. L knew it was worth the wait!

Part 2

Rose near the Lodges of the Sea on planet earth nearby the gate to Dorthrin. Grown up in one of the richest families of Superbia within a family of creatures, beasts and shrubberies with only one pair of socks and one pair of shoes. When the Halflings grew up they slightly wanted to commit suicide for missing their parents while growing up to become grown-ups. Their beastly nanny's came in just in time to prevent them for committing suicide. After this coincidence they thought the twins a wisely lesson on how to prevent them from committing suicide ever again by generously aiding them with XTC-pills they had to take once a month. A couple years later before their adulthood they got caught in hostage due to a crime they convicted. They stole diamonds and accessories from expensive stores not knowing that they truest came from a richly family. After a couple of years with some skilled criminal years pooled with liquor and drugs they reconciled their life with the love for their musical and artistic talent for playing the piano and guitar. Regaining their supremacy to save children who where victims of pedophiles and participated in the game of chess in their beastly pack of wolves and other enchantments.

It was both their parents who left trails behind to accomplish this talent. In their younger years the twins even learned how to steal by some demons from the deepest fires from hell. They once committed a crime with this ability by using stolen money to buy a CD inspired by *Beethoven* to listen to their melody. This mission was learnt from sinful civilians and was never repeated again after shrubberies and creatures found out about this charter. The entire action of robbing stores. This wasn't necessary but it was the raisers who wanted to be on familiar terms with how they would develop themselves in both worlds, the civilized world and that of the purgatory world and hell to see if they would commit crimes and how they would befall. A game.

After some time the Halflings got a regular job to buy everything they ever wanted and to stay undercover occupied while being raised by fantastic creatures and beasts and shrubberies, their part-time job was to slaughter demons and sinners besides their civilized lives, just like their parents did when they were still part of Dorthrin. In their free time they grew stronger while Uriela would play the piano and Raphael the guitar. Their strength grew into astonishing famous supremacy that no pedophile ever came to existence on planet earth and got vanished from earth and doomed in hell under the eyes of Satan and his workforce. Some tried to come back as enlightened entities to revenge upon the Halflings. Some not. Afraid to lose a fruitless dooming battle against the highest supremacy. All believers of L and S got pretty impressed by the work their Halflings achieved in the factory of killing and slaughtering demons and sinners on a daily basis. With killing demons the twins gained some fees to buy themselves some music equipment and formed a music group with other fantastic beasts to get music from the ground into the human world.

Unfortunately the other beasts left the group due to low interest and other tone keys that wouldn't match with the sound that the Halflings where aiming for.

During university in Dorthrin the Halflings where made fun of because of their practices and they had to figure out a name to name their music album. They got inspired by a horror movie from *Freddy Kruger* and continued to score high hopes with their talents.

The Halflings performed on stages in the civilized world like truest artists proved to amuse the halls of human fame with their talent. Until they came to a point where one of their fans threw a demonic dick on stage. The Halflings thought it was a meat sausage and Uriela took a bite of the sausage. It wasn't a meat sausage, it was a penis of a demonic pedophile and Uriela realized this afterwards that it was a real dick. It was a remembrance thrown by a rival who had high hopes that a new deadly plague would return as a revenge of a world with many new broken children by pedophiles haunted in both worlds once Satan wouldn't take over the guidance in hell. Wondering who was the fan in the crowed that threw it? With what reason? Where did he get this penis? There could only be one answer to it. A demonic Giant.

Part 3

In the deepest fires of hell doom giants. Giants dooming from hell, are at times remarkable in strength and size. Fairytales like *Jack the Giant Killer* have formed the modern perception of giants as foolish and cruel ogres. Sometimes known of eating demonic human souls, while other giants tend to eat beasts and creatures. Some giants in dooming hell are both intelligent and friendly just like in tales as *Roald Dahl*. Giants in hell outside Dorthrin, that in times cross Superbia, a village in Dorthrin, represent the human body enlarged to the point of being monstrous. Giants stir up fear and remind humans of their imperfection and mortality. Giants are immortal but grow to a certain extend. The giants from hell. They are monsters, but the Halflings found some exceptions. There once was a giant that mingled with the lives in Dorthrin in a friendly way and could even be seen as part of beastly, shrubbery, creaturely family with its immortality as a Halfling's giant friend.

Hundreds of mighty, and somewhat gigantic, heroes, and friendly war elephants from hell have died by Satan's catch. Giant demons are the watchers workforce under Satan's command. Some giants were handsome, with curly hair, sparkling eyes and strong arms. Among the giants, the Halflings friend, he was the bravest and most famous. He was a friend of all who later was chosen by the twins to become absolute ruler over the giants and heroes including enemies in hell. Giants created regular games in the deepest flames of hell. Gaints are rough but generally righteous of formidable strength living in caves.

Demonic giants decide to stick to a
lifestyle in the forests in hell.
Sometimes holding a secret and
wisdom unknown to the lives of
demons and sinners in hell
alongside their most outstanding
feature, their length. That one giant.
As Halflings friendly giant lived in
the mountains of hell, fed itself on
raw meat and often fought against
dragons. All giants were afraid of
blackberries among the glooming
shrubberies that poised a danger of
making the giants mushroom-trip
and die, so they offered sacrifices to
those shrubberies in hell. There are
giants who play with ships moving
them from one port to another. In
hell giants are able to crush demons
with their feet and when laying
down to sleep they can be so long as
their body reaches from the
volcanoes mountains to the flaming
forest. Some giants are black bulls

belonging to the underdogs of Satan's watchers and some belong to certain volcanoes in hell.

The Halflings where somewhat decent visiting their giant friend often and offered it snakes. They were doomed once by being involved in a battle within the giant game with an Olympian demonic giant. A friendly giant appeared before the demon could attack the twins. This conflict was eventually settled when the giant hero decided to help. He became their armor of darkness.

There are forest giants, fire giants, and mountain giants. The most various monsters go against each other in gaming battles in hell, and in the eventual battle, the giants will storm and fight against demonic workforce assistants of Satan until the underworld is destroyed and rebuild again.

Even so, the demonic entities themselves were related to many marriages. There are also such who have good relationships with hell and bear little difference in status to them. The great grandson of Lucifer. The entire world of demons in hell was created from the flesh of Satan's workforces and a giant who's considered to be consuming cocaine in the after schools or work activities wasn't being punished by dooming hell, he was a monstrous sinner after all.

Once upon a moment in time the friendly giant consisted of a pack and they came in two, they all had a partner in life. A friendly giant man and woman at that time existed. They were traveling to a *Dragon Island* with their pets when the man lost their wife and their pet, to their surprise they stepped into the bright rays of daylight. As a result of exposure to daylight, all woman and pets were turned into rocks. He and a few others were left alone without an other half. Moved themselves from the rocks on earth to the dooming world in hell.

Their wives turned out to be red headed giants. The red-haired giants are beautiful cannibalistic giants who live in hell in the rocky mountains. After giving birth to a child, the giants treated the child so poorly that Satan responded by making his lands flaming hot and gloomy and allowing rivals to defeat the friendly giants pack, which killed them all in the dooming flames and kept only a few friendly giants that remained under the eyes among fellows that were cruel and made him shrink upon a certain height. Only a few male giants survived the game. Those who survived, their skin became pale for eternally living in the fires of hell.

The few giants that were left were crowned, defeated in their own lands in hell and depicted as snakes. They were restricted in some parts of hell. Giants built mountains on planet earth. High *stone town* walls and *rock city's* that are seen on earth are the creation of giants. Giants create beautiful landscapes. Giants dug a channel around the Dandelion field until they reach the village in Droplet Cloud, splitting the guide into two separate waterways with one leading through the forest. Other giants threw up rocks, or became rocks themselves when they touched with light and died on the spot. Most Giants were evil beings that threatened, robbed and killed travelers of hell and in between the

fires of hell, such as Dorthrin.
Medieval giants are cronies of
Satan's workforce. Except for one
giant.

The sleeping giant only awakens if a
specific musical instrument is
played near the fires of hell. The
guitarist and the pianist. Most giants
are stupid. A demonic giant who
had wrangled a demonic soul in hell
went to bury it in a village with dirt.
However, the friendly giant met a
clothes maker, varying clothes to
repair, and the clothes convinced the
giant that he had worn out all the
clothes coming from demons. Giants
throw gemstones, used to explain
many great gemstones in the
landscapes in the deepest fires of
hell. Giants are mostly gigantic. The
Halflings have a new friend. A
friendly giant who lives in the
mountains in the deepest fires of
hell, carrying a giant unconditional

mountain lovingly spirit on planet earth. He is a true hero to them teaching them the creation of demonic vampire spells. A friend.

Part 4

The stage. With this incident the twins had to go to an institution. With some luck they got unrestricted from this prison institution from a good cup who happened to be a demonic beastly wolf friend living among humanity in the civilized world as an officer of the highest rank. After going to prison, all paparazzi where all over the Halflings questioning where the real black blood was from and if they noticed they were biting a dead man's dick. Once the Halflings were drunk they even almost ate a vampires heart during a night out after performing on stage in the civilized world. The blood would stream all over the stage and over the fans on front row. The twins were pulled out of the stage by force and handcuffed behind the stages to be entering a bad cup car to be brought back into the police cell for further investigation. Their parents were wolves that could survive in 30 days without vampire tear but by the light of the moon and 3 days without transformation or a heart. The investigation didn't take longer than expected in the civilized world by the good officer. He knew they had to guzzle.

The time of bright moon was a wicked period for the Halflings. The twins got married with their demonic ghost friends and their demonic best friends survived dooming hell. The Halflings were completely cultivated by this insight. Although it might seem that the twins want to kill as some Giants do, remember that they only did this once they where influenced under drugs and alcohol that lead to an addiction and eventually to their depression in the deepest fires of hell. The victory of their addiction to cocaine, MDMA-crystals and weed was beyond their bravery by the help and guidance of visiting the giants that sent them on a secretly adventure. In hell the Halflings feasted on drugs and liquor and they consumed so much that they created imaginary friends that were their delusional friends that gave them visional tasks to forget their parents and kill every imprint of them that comes along their path.

Their demonic friendly Giant friends, not all of them were friendly, grabbed the Halflings and put them in the dungeon in the mountains of dooming hell. To give them some time. Time for them to rethink what they did wrong and to quite the alcohol and drug abuse for a while.

The twins regained their strengths to get out of the addicted life in the civilized world that led to their time in prison and to let go of MDMA-crystals and stick to cocaine and *vodka red-bull*, they had more love for their lovers, and rose to the top by the guidance of a friendly giant. They regained their life back on earth with the acceptance to get doomed out of the flames of hell with scars remaining in the purgatory fires of Dorthrin, and would be forever marked for the creatures and shrubberies to always remember that they considered going to walk through the dooming fires of hell. But little did the creatures and shrubberies and other beasts know and the humans on planet earth showed that it was a miracle from the giant to help the Halflings seek a gateway from hell to let them rise out of hell where there is no rest for the wicked.

After there where no more tears shed in the Sea by the demonic enlightened entities and the lightened entities in hell would live loudly in the mores and would slowly turn into dust by the hand of the demonic giants who swallowed the lost entities with their tools into darkened hell where they would live and feast with the evil giants who became the leaders in hell that were appointed by Satan.

There were giant feasts is whereupon the twins were invited to attend. With their wounds and scars they could travel through 3 worlds. Only the Halflings could do. Nor their parents neither the divines nor enchantments from Dorthrin Firegale would ever dare. Afraid they would never get back from hell back to the purgatory world. Not only would they feast in hell, but also down to earth with humans that they grew up with during their evolution. They would celebrate their return in Dorthrin for the mistake they made in drugs and love for falling for a nightmare. The ghostly friends, that become lovers and ended becoming everything to them where doomed in hell with joyfulness and ecstasy and their soul became slowly enlightened in the Seas mores. Changes. The Halflings belonged more to Dorthrin and had to leave planet earth and all their friends and richness that they inherited from their parents. Not that Dorthrin wasn't that richly inherited, but more wicked. The change they made by making the crossroad to hell made them more lithe to travel to the dooming fires and meet their new demonic friendly giant and to consume on demons heart tear, if they had a heart. They had to feed. Feeding themselves while under protection of the giants. Being unseen on planet earth for the humans by catching the wondering demons by 4PM and in Dorthrin independently. After recovering from drug abuse in their nightmares from hell they had to let go of the giant. They simply got fired. The firing rains turned into black like the black colors of the piano keys. The demonic giants withheld their stage as leaders and *Rasputin* took over the dooming fires of the nightmares of hell. The evil giants found a replacer in the dooming flames to lead over the lost souls of demonic sinners, evil murderers and suicidal accidental malevolent humans including innocent beasts, creatures and captured the poisons shrubberies that were kept hostage. The Halflings found a new adventure. To release and free the citizens that were kept hostage of all the villages belonging to Dorthrin like Superbia and bring them back to purgatory realm. The Halflings saved their friends from the dooming nightmares of hell. Under the graveyard on earth ending into empty graves. To set free souls that went straight to hell shall be relieved in dreams and clouds of the humans on planet earth that lost their loved ones that took the flight that was cursed by *Rasputin*.

Part 5

Remembrance, awakening for the return of loved ones on earth. Some darkened homes plan a funeral without a body in the civilized world. On the airplane is the least where we ever think of death upon us. Traveling over sea is a good way to go. Universal standards are seen as bumpy, furrowed, dangerous, stiff and squeaky. Most demonic humans prefer traveling by car close by earth others mostly by air, seeming poky and reliably limited publicly rather than with a jet.

A flight over the Sea above waters what lies above the deepest fires of hell, deeper than Dorthrin Firegale, other than Superbia. There happen deadly disasters. Airplanes go missing from the radar. Some of such planes carry passengers from all walks of life, children that steal or lie, mothers who sin, grandfathers who sin, husbands and wives who carry secrets. It's a wonder that these flights don't carry babies along. Babies' soul's that die shall survive the flames of Lucifer by the power of their innocence. Airplanes missing in the misty clouds from heavy sea and even calm waters with family's of whom little children's experiencing their first traveling heading back home from boarding school. Swarming clouds and insecure weather. Most victims trapped inside the steel as the plane goes down. Nobody would recover from the sky tomb that would get caught in the inescapable waters of the Sea. The deadliest flight.

The water of the Sea is always smooth seeming not dangerous. The few planes passing over the sea always go missing. Among those few there is always a list of those humanly sinners that committed crimes and lived a humanly life full sins. Most of the passengers are humans that "redrum", are suicidal or try to commit suicide. It starts with a strange groovy motion that is felt by the pilot. Some first class passengers dive out of the plane into the water and start swimming for the shore alongside the stewards and stewardesses. Less lucky.

Second class mostly can't escape less tragic and aren't able to make the jump clearly. Trapping hundreds of passengers in the back wing of the plane once it goes missing. Passengers' trying to breath the remaining air once the plane hits the water and drowns from the opened door from the first class. Many human souls of dead woman, children and old people are visible in the Sea. Visible as demonic entities envisioned as lights of the dead with souls that need to be released from the skyline tomb. Humanly passengers finding a desperate effort to escape. Trying to find an opening for oxygen. Alive but sentenced to death in lost demonic bodies and souls. Darkened homes with wandering souls in the civilized world with full moon and once the darkness strikes. Trapped in steel in remembrance of loved ones on earth to pay their darkest sin.

The Halflings Raphael and Uriela found a few visionary demonic friends, some new demonic ghost creatures. These entities got stuck between both worlds. The world of Dorthrin and that of the deepest fires of hell, the demonic world. They were fantastic ghost friends. Some boys and girls trying to grip an opening towards the brighter fires. Instead of letting go they, and other boys and girls swam freely before the airplane completely disappeared and sank. Others tried to drag them down and called them to set them free. To free them at last took some time for themselves. This plane was different. These fantastic creature ghost friends were special to be met by the Halflings. That something special was that there was no list available of any sinful human passenger on board of the plane what made this accident a mystical ghost plane. They were squeezed to death among humans if not drowned to death by the hand of the Sea its destiny. No matter whoever jumped off the plane into the Sea towards the deepest fire of hell. First class or second. All got eaten by the wildlife of hell's life in the Sea, demonic meat-eating-fish and crocodiles, and not to forget demonic snakes in the Sea. The demonic entity boy and girl friends, that were a lost soul, told the Halflings, who adored danger in Hell with water sports by the Sea, to make sure to get on the darn board as fast as possible or stay out of the water. The Halflings knew they were windsurfing on enlightened lost souls from hell.

Local demons sentenced to hell near the Sea were abandoned to consume from the Sea. Laughter and seduces of the demons remained to twitch pulling and cutting out more parts of decomposed bodies to feed and to deliver souls from the bottom of the Sea to Satan. In the civilized world the bodies were never found and souls lay brightened out in the darkness with elegance over the Sea for identification by a pilot of the second catastrophic flight to travel over the sea. A following tragic happening with indescribable sinful deaths.

By following the crows and other plants from Dorthrin Firegale were guidance for the Halflings as an enchanting from the parents S and L to find helpless lost souls hit by accidental sinners guided by the stand of the moon.

Part 6

A moment on earth before December the 12th of 2012

With this letter I write to you my beloved child to reach out to you before you go to sleep or whenever you get the chance to read this. I wrote this and reached out to you while it is in the middle of the night... I am surrounded by darkness, I live within the complete fading of the light. And no, the shaking of my body isn't caused by the darkness. It is he. Your father. I can feel him, although I can't see him. I feel it. I feel him. In every portion of his body, in al his nerves I can feel him. He sneaks up on me. He demands me, although he doesn't even touch me. I am completely handed over to him, naked on my knees, in the middle of a soft woolen carpet in the sky. Strong hands hold my knees together close to my thighs, and another pair of loose hands hold my chest tight with my arms to the back. It hurts as a human, on a bittersweet, thrilling way. Although I am lifted there naked and vulnerable, I know by now that these things turn me on in a way that I never ever could've imagined. It's completely illogical, I feel deadly because I don't know his every move, but still I yearn for his ever tizzy movement. And I am so afraid for the moment that I have to kneel for him in the darkness. Afraid because I have so less control over my body's reaction, because he completely owns me on places I don't even know about myself, but when I am with him, I become what he wants me to be for him. I become his willingly queen, even if I know I'm just a beauty in his known chess game. He has promised me that he will own me. He will never be the same for me as I'm for him. I shall never own him, the same way that he owns me. I shall play according to his rules and I shall never get to know how the rules

shall change. What move or how shall
the game begin into a new game, as I
call these intimate reunions. And
yesterday, when there was a spotlight
shining right at me and only at me, once
he stepped out of the darkness and stood
in front of me, it was the manly wolf
who stood next to me who touched me
deep inside of me. Change. I had to do
this. But there last night, in that room I
wasn't L. I was just his property.
Sometimes, in the morning glory, if he
can't touch me, if we're not together, I
think I want to be myself sometimes,
that I can be L again. But I don't
remember who that is anymore. I'm not
quite sure if I know myself any longer.
Who is L? Your mother, L.

The Halflings were smothered in a
tunnel of complete darkness in one
of the Lodges on the beaches of the
Sea, that was caused by a surprising

power breakage in the rooms, where
they were digging for information
out the previous life of their mother
L who happened to have an other
name, Queen M, their mother that
could help them to find themselves.
The twins found themselves in the
middle of one or another horror
movie, the kind of that you don't
want to see like *The Grudge*, and they
saw themselves as the *Girl* and *Boy*
that constantly does the wrong
things and will result in a bloody
end the more they get to know about
their parents, their mothers past.
They were living in vain. Everybody
on Earth is talking about her death
and in Dorthrin they say she was a
true enchantment and that both
Halflings have her looks. Well, that
is what the shrubberies and the
creatures keep telling Uriela and
Raphael. Uriela, she adores logical
feelings and loves herself for the fear

that her mother leaves her in that is almost rational.

This was one of the few power breakages where the sea above hell is dealing with that lead to an accident caused by an airplane for a long time. The worst that the twins could have ever overcome is that there is a demonic mouse crawling on the surfboard while wind surfing over the Sea...

"The damned cursing winter" said Raphael after a long silence and he shoved the empty whiskey bottle over the bar near the Sea, where he spent his late mornings. "What problem haven't we already experienced with this dirty cocaine! And how many will we get..."

It was late, beside him there came into sight surprisingly someone else at the bar that only he could catch a glimpse of, alone at a table she sat, in the half darkness barely recognizable shadows, a girl, that was reading the newspaper and was pretending to eat her breakfast. She replied, "You think this is the only dirty cocaine you can get around here? Or is it just because you're to used to the same supplier around here and you hear nothing about them others". She said without looking at him, Raphael. This was how Raphael met his demonic girlfriend ghost at the bar near the Sea.

The Halflings are most precious beasts. They can feed on earth, hell and Dorthrin other than their parents who could only be fed by demons from hell. Other than their demonic ghostly friends, they don't eat. Their demonic friends, they are being eaten by demonic creatures from The Sea together with evil giants that hunt on their enlightened souls with their tools. They belong more and more to hell and get slashed away from the world of enlightened entities and slowly fade away from the lightest fires of hell. Besides heart tears and pedophilic dicks, on earth, the Halflings guzzle mostly flesh. They eat meat from cows, goats and sheep. They do have some kind of diet though. They don't guzzle wild animals, fish and chicken. In the past they refused to eat from purgatory villages like baby beasts and creatures. Now they guzzle porridge consisting of eggs of all sorts of animals that lay eggs. They don't eat much fruit or vegetables. The Halflings still remain healthy. In summer and spring seasons, if demons produce devilish milk, they drink it with blood from vampires sometimes. To let a demonic vampire's blood is sort of a tradition they learnt from other creatures and beasts from hell that had to guzzle in the deepest fires of hell while being kept prisoners. They search for a healthy demonic vampire in the earthly crowd or a wanderer in Superbia. They fasten the finger of with a wedding ring. Than the Halfling who fetched the demon shoots it with their silver bullet gun in the neck of the vampire. The thirst of their blood is being fetched in a calabash. If the Halflings catches more than a liter they squeeze the wound close of the demonic vampire, to make the bleeding stop and after the demon is being released among the other demonic humans and vampire pack of demons on earth they mark them with a burning scar of a cross of the Lord Jesus Christ by the flames of hell. The Halflings could drink their blood without turning into a newborn. They were twins of emperors. A demon from hell and demonic vampire doesn't remorse to lose more than a liter of blood. The Halflings give them a mark after their fed and keep in mind that the same daemon doesn't have to bleed again within the next four moons, the Halflings mingle their milk with demonic blood and drink it. They love sweet things. Sweet things. Halflings mingle Dorthrin magical milk with divine creatures urine to take out the poison from hell in their bloody drink. That's how they prevent to become newborns. They also collect creatures' honey from divine ground-bees. They are a lot superior to regular earthly bees and they sting. Their honey is deep under the ground near hell close to Superbia. The movements of the shrubberies are gently hollowing out the honey.

Part 7

A touch from the skies on bear feet
as L awakens thinking of her truest
beloved children living and playing
in Dorthrin and on planet earth. The
eyes never felt such brightness and
safety from heaven upon earth
together with her truest beloved
now known as the king in heaven, S.
Both have known mermaids in
heaven who guides them to eternal
ecstasy and all forms of heavenly
lives. Within all lives of heaven there
are equally standings like in
Dorthrin but less malicious and
sinful.

It was almost the moment and time
that the birds would start to sing in
the morning whilst in Dorthrin the
birds would warn all Superbia for
fires of hell to flame harder. To
unreached the grounds of Superbia
divines. In heaven there is no such

thing. In heaven L and S only see what their heart yearns to lovingly catch a glimpse of their most tenderly memories in their lives. For L this was the moment that S came into her life and created two wunderkind of their own. Both wonder how their lives are on planet earth on which they as parents can overlook the situation but the sight of what happens in Dorthrin and further is foggily and not to follow or get hold on.

The Halflings Raphael and Uriela, live a simple life without parents but they do have natural powers to imprint their parents thoughts and other supernatural powers that protects them from danger and the other way around. They are children of a famous rockstar on planet earth and a famous pianist. Moreover, they never have to spend time to meet their parents and especially if they don't have to communicate with the demons from hell. The entire situation changes when their demonic ghost friends, who happen to be intelligent, smart and tremendously generous and gorgeous wake up the Halflings every single morning on the beaches near the Sea with lively rock music after some nightly fireplaces with firework and demonic meat.

The Halflings are free at last, after a complicated start they held a grip and a chance to start their own business on planet earth within the richest families in the universe.

All of a sudden the twins were doomed to lose their jobs as freelancers once they made a mistake by letting in some unwanted demonic enemies into their houses. They invited their demonic ghostly friends into their houses and created with them a venture, a giant's job with severe creatures, animals and shrubberies staying between severe planets, that happened to bring them to a newly adventure. The demonic ghosts were steamy half naked strangers with an indifferent attitude of a real lady and gentleman who helped them get the job done, making them included, and tremendously nervous once the demonic ghosts showed secretly interest in the twins doomed from hell.

The first date after the conversations at the bar led for the demonic ghost girlfriend to arrive in a trench coat with stockings and tremendously inflaming lingerie. She wanted to amaze Raphael and show him devotion. He has always wanted to start something with a lady he can truest trust. Is this demonic ghostly girl the only distinction of the rule?

Knowing that one day she would fade away and that he would end up without a lover…

The nerve-breaking look of Raphael betrayed his love feelings and secret about the incident with his girlfriend in front of her sister Uriela once she arrived in her trench coat and their ghost boyfriend was visiting at that time, having their secret magical cocaine party for four. Well that is what the twins thought but apparently the demonic ghostly girlfriend did not see this. She expected a night with just the two of them. The party where he made love under influence of cocaine, witnessed by his twin sister and her demonic ghost friend. He and his demonic ghostly girlfriend had to leave and run away from them. There was more to the story why they had to escape that is what

Uriela and her ghost friend knew.
There was no other way.

Part 8

After ten years of service in the mystic world and deputy of *Lucifer*, S was ready for his white history, and his crown, to restart his new ritual as a high-end undercover agent heavenly spirit on earth. The only thing that doesn't let him rest his case peacefully in heaven is the situation that he killed himself for love that caused him a one-man task from the Lord and God to fulfill near the Sea above Dorthrin. He had to find a companion in the fellowship nearby the Sea to start a new investigation of the cause of his suicide action that might be related to the accident of the crashed ghost airplane that disappeared of the radar with no passengers list. With his new companion nearby the Sea above Dorthrin he started a cocktail bar nearby the waters of the Sea with the thought of the fulfillment of his one man job, little did they know in heaven was that S had a phoenix as a guided friend to overlook the visions in Dorthrin, villages and hell. As everyone knows, S is a clever agent, and is aware over every move from hell and is fully warned before anything happens to him or his loved ones on planet earth, hell or Superbia except for heaven, heaven is heavenly safe. He fulfilled his duty as an undercover agent from heaven with the eyes upon hell that nobody could envision coming from a heavenly spirit on earth that was sent of from above.

Uriela noticed something wrong with her demonic ghostly girlfriend who happened to be a really breezy ghostly lady girl coming from an exotic country. Everything she knows about the gorgeous exotic girl with a cute eyewear, is that she used to be a hardworking single from *Afrique* who happened to travel on the flight on her way to her minor from school. But she thinks to recognize something in her eyes... Uriela, she thinks that both, her brother and she, fell in love with each other and Uriela, she could tell by the ghost her green flaming eyes. Usually they are flaming red. There is something weird with how she looked at her brother her twin brother left on an international flight.

Young and spoiled. The ghost, she told Uriela and her brother that before her tragic death, long before the airplane accident she had a student life for the rest of her life. Besides, she had a glooming career as a writer before she became a dancer and before she met Raphael at the bar. She also had a girlfriend that was on the previous flight. Both met on the airport, and felt connected the moment they met. She was somewhat bisexual. There was no doubt, that the moment she met Raphael in the bar that both belonged together. She was sure she found the one that she was longing for and to whom she belonged. Once she met Raphael she found the one she was searching for. She enjoyed every single moment with him and everything was a new experience with him. "The day that I fell for your brother, the boy that I felt directly connected with, the handsome rockstar child from a famous guitarist. The thought made me explode. I felt like I had everything I ever wanted." She told Raphael his sister.

Egoistic. Uriela, she showed her ghost manly travel companion her body during a trip on the yacht. That is where she met him sexually poisonously. She fell in love with him in a storm of deadly passion and romance. A clumsy night it was. Bumping on his chin. She couldn't stand the seduction, but had to deal with the sabotages of the love of their relationship, the thought of his fading and disappearance. Both ended up with secrets to one another. They didn't tell what they felt about their intimacy and their clumsiness that evening after the party when the demonic ghostly boyfriend sent her the *Whatsapp*. In the period when he left, after she exploded and expressed her love by making love, he turned secretly against the Halfling's feeling by expressing himself playing with her powers by a fatale kiss that grew his power. Uriela, her talent by playing the piano gave her in turn new power up until her demonic ghostly friend became a pianist too because his friend is a guitarist and she, Uriela is a pianist too. But this life of all four, would it ever be satisfying for the Halflings, for them all together or apart, or would they eventually always long for the goodness of their feelings or the evil for eternally imprinted death? In sickness and in health until their lovingly friends fade away... There was need of a voyage.

Richness. A secretly lonely pianist yearning for her mothers imprint returning back to the village where it all started, Droplet Cloud in the fields of Dandelions surrounded with waters. Slowly inflaming by the demonic guzzling with hallucinations of hells living, back to being free. A pianist who looked forward to and entirely new adventure in totally new worlds surrounded in opportunities to fulfill her secret dream, the discovery like *Columbus*. A talented and genius life. Longing for answers to her mother's letters that she left behind. The twins' piano inherited from their mother was ruined during a burglar daylight by demons, bringing both Halflings, back to the secrets of their mothers' letters. Both can't admit the obsessive feelings they have for the lives of their parents, their history has left love and many scars behind that become more and more debatable to the Halflings and they both admit that their love and passion no longer go hand in hand. As a pianist and guitarist both know they play with fire but their sins are to intriguing to accept that they are meant to take care of each other, nor apart but in hell. By surviving the rumors from the demons that stand

between their love that money cant
buy them happiness in hell, they
quiet didn't get the picture of what
kind of divine and fantastic beasts
the Halflings both can turnout to be.
Created by S and L and can
transform into a beast above Satan
and leader to all in the darkest fires
if, both choose for brother and sister
love in the darkest part of the entire
creation. The flames of dooming
hell.

Traitor. Both twins wonder, about
their darkest side to protect their
relation, both realize that their own
passion in love for one another
might be self destructive for both
sides. She could've been as much as
a virgin living in a lonely world on
her way to hell. Under the eyes of
Satan, her love was on a rise. But a
new world, a new sensation, and
new seduces, and it doesn't take
much time or she ends up in a

dangerous situation with intrigues and desires that she thought to had left behind. In the meantime, her love, her darkened brother, Raphael is frustrated by her intendance at the Seas bar presentation about the penalty of him going to hell. He decides to follow his ghost girlfriend's path because he can't live any longer without her presence if she would ever fade away. What the Halflings don't know is that their secretly devotion towards their demonic friends is a spy contract from hell. The more they get attached to their demonic ghostly friends the more power they loose against Satan. There was a need of a plan by the twins.

The demonic *Afrique* ghost entity, alongside her girlfriend Uriela, both have been named many things, "Whore, slut!" and so on. But little did they know that the Halflings had a forbidden book with which they could curse their graves and make those humans belong to the lost souls.

Part 9

After an adventure, Uriela, the badass girl dressed in *Prada* on earth, had been named after many things during the summer sun. There had been no given name that ever described her reputation that she actually earned. Her only matter was to make sure she is perfectly dressed in masterpiece high fashion *haute-couture* clothing's from the foundation that her parents left behind and to take care of her perfect figure including sharing her private jet, earned from their parents, with her brother Raphael and have fun with their exotic ghost friends and others.

But Raphael is everything except happy. His plan to escape from his sister. He expects a child with the *African beauty* and has no time for partying or fun stuff anymore with his twin sister and his demonic ghost friend met at the Sea. Uriela, the last girl that came out of the wound of her mother, decides to no longer hang around with her ghost friend from Afrique. Instead she decides to live a life alone with someone unknown in Dorthrin, not knowing that a demon is on the strike. A demon that had a relation with her parents and unfinished business with them.

So once Raphael asks the Afrique ghost friend to go out, she grabs her chances and goes on a date with the charming divine. A while ago his sister, Uriela, thought that Raphael was interleaving playboy manners, to avoid her requests to have some fun at the Sea, Uriela suddenly decided to go on a wild weekend trip to Dorthrin. There she meets his brother again, in a dark, seductive and extremely dangerous businessman alike that knows exactly how to treat her little sister...

Where both were, would always be their home. It was about that time that both would lay the next steps and prove themselves that both were fully aware of what their plans where. For always.

A sudden meeting in Dorthrin changed in a romance once Uriela decides to move together with her ghostly boyfriend on a family site on earth. Her brother and her exotic ghostly girlfriend had other plans on how to get married together. With the lovingly support of the *Rafiki* beasts, and with the recent discovery that the ghosts also have relatives living there, Uriela could finally release the tragic family endeavors, between her and her brother, of him being a entertainer, and let her past behind and set her first footsteps to a colorful future.

On the family site on earth there is something that endangers the situation.

Although the wolves pack, creatures and shrubberies, a family of fantastic, thinks that both Halflings desires the side of hell, it is pretty clear that both astonishing divine demonic ghost friends don't wholeheartedly love the Halflings as a friend or more sexual wise but, more as enemies. And than there is Raphael, the mystic and handsome brother, that tells her sister what uplifts him from demonic male ghost and the wolves pack, the past of the Halflings parents started unflustered. Shocking truths about their parent's death are being revealed during a Dorthrin gathering, in the life of the happiest couples that will change their lives forever.

Whoever really delves into the lives of L and S, who achieved something in Dorthrin and on earth understands their championships of their achievements.

Rumors are the most favorite occupation in Dorthrin but the parents of the Halflings knew pretty well how to keep their secrets safe.

Eight years ago before L and S ever got married, S had a relationship with an incredibly rich girl that he didn't love in Dorthrin. There was a future where he didn't want to be part of. The only way to escape the planned marriage was to escape. Escape by giving power with what he was born with, by simply giving up. And that was exactly his plan, at the end of the summer he would step into his Jaguar and speedily never look back.

This was before he met the beautiful enchanted divine L.

The twins father S, and their mother L. It started as an innocent love in their youngest years when they could write in Latin at the age of seven and eight, once she was a twenty something year old girl that isolated herself from the rest of the world and was famous, rich and beyond beautiful that no man could barely not fall in love, was the moment that their father decided to marry her. She became the daughter of *Medusa*. She didn't come into sight in the same social circles in the civilized world. Nobody knew that they used to be friends, let alone lovers. But during the winter, the twenty something year old girl became the most important girl to S in the entire universe from heaven to hell.

S, he could abandon his plans. He had to leave planet earth, but he decided to come back for her, L.

If he decides to return after years being apart from her in between years, later than promised, he thinks he is too late. A demonic vampire from Satan from Paris had seduced his girl of his dreams and future wife...

Uriela felt the imprint from her father to his mother

"When you were away

It seemed like the prettiest goodbye

In fire and flame

When you came back

You were mine" was imprinted in whispers in the twin's ears going straight to their beating hearts from S to L.

Part 10

Before deciding to travel by flight towards a land of magical wonders, it was during a freezing winter. The ghostly friends of the twins had a dream.

During their flight they crossed a manly passenger, a sinner who almost freeze to death… The girl and the boy assisted to help but all they could do is give him an airplane blanket to keep him warm from the cold… he died eventually from the accident on their way to a land of wonders…

During the international flight over the sea to a land of wonders the pilot took a pause at a village, Droplet Cloud… The flight went missing.

Before the plane went missing the ghost girl and ghost boy woke up from a long sleep in the cold air…

some passengers crucified their belongings on the Christ peak that was on board... The ghost boy and girl had to take their belongings down from the peak and inform the passengers that their belongings aren't doomed and don't cause harm on this plane...

Once their belongings were released from the cross they decided to leave the airplane as soon as possible once landed on their final destination. They came across a wolf without notice. The wolf was fast and was on the haunt for a demonic creature on the flight. The demonic creature ran darn fast but little did it know that the wolf was faster and that he was trapped in a cabin of sinners. The flight was doomed. Luckily the wolves came in packs and consisted of a strong crew. They lost track when boarding at Droplet Cloud

and the demon got away in the
forest during the pause.

On the international flight in the
cold winter, the ghosts met this
soldier who accepted them as grown
ups, thought them how to consume
liquor and sniff cocaine on the plane.
You have to experience consuming
alcohol and drugs once you've been
in the military army with this guy...
The ghosts envision his shinny red
nose... Both ghosts coming from an
elite would've got highly ranked
into their army after his lesson... It'll
take some time to be accepted in the
military with those two addictions,
so the ghost boy and girl spend their
money and time in the most elegant
flight...

Part 11

The Halflings saw all sorts of
consumable heart tear possible
sinners, demonic vampires,
damageable pedophiles from
outside their corridors… a few
meters further was a sea with mostly
entities from the deepest fires of hell
that they at first wanted to play with
and eventually kill by taking a shot
of cocaine and later consume the
demonic wonderers with their
beasty companions, shrubbery meat-
eaters and creaturely families who
came to visit their palace in Dorthrin
Firegale and near the Sea, but
instead they found better heart meat
to guzzle… a pedophilic pig with a
dick meat attached to a string that
apparently got swallowed by the
first pedophile and digested
instantly and consumed by the
second pedophile and so on… the
catch was heavy to carry to bring a

fresh dinner to the table… no water sport was lacking that would shower them with fame, if they wanted to appease generosity, like pearls strung on a string…

The demonic pedophiles were so heavy that they could carry the Halflings and make them fly and jump a few meters off their feet… Good advice is expensive, but not too expensive to them! Because although they hadn't the slightest idea of their destination they knew how to maneuver from demons, that they remained straight home to Superbia…

They directly flew themselves into the kitchen with demonic pedophiles on the furnace and with luck to them the heat of the demonic chef friend wasn't on…

Some sinners, demonic vampires, pedophiles caught by the power of the Halflings, they got away… this time they decided to use their magical guns with silver and golden bullets… the guns were a gift received by precious enchanted warriors while the presence of their imprinted minds from their parents S and L was kept as a real secret. As real divine warriors they gifted this to their children, the Halflings, as an offer to owe to their survival to an incident that once took place to never forget the power of their father and mother.

During the Halflings playing field they nailed a demonic white fox from hell on a shrubbery tree… the fur was too precious to be ruined by a magical bullet… Folks! What a fur! Sometimes we can correct a mistake by sheer luck…

So many shrubberies, beasts and creatures… even a wild lost demonic pedophile with no network that was old and demented that the Halflings played with was carried to bring to the table… the females among the pedophiles can sometimes behave very badly to children, but the males are much more ferocious…

A child that once got hit by a malevolent pedophile in the forest recognized the Halflings. For the child's mind, it became imprinted in a *Déjà-vu*… the twins thought, wouldn't a baby human rather use any imagination of no means rather than accept a disaster?

An evil vampire pack at the borders of Dorthrin once attacked the Halflings, while their guns were running out of bullets… They figured how to make a silver bomb and blew up the vampire pack but this was a way of how the story could end for the pack of vampires. Instead the twins they chose to climb themselves into a shrubbery tree and wait for the vampires to go away to hell…

With luck they found a sable with which they could attach their jacket and swing a cross of the Lord Christ towards their soulless body part… they went away crawling backwards… it seemed like fate was following the Halflings! They encountered the most dangerous scenarios, the ones they're the least prepared for on their journey to evolution…

The airplane flight sank! It wasn't the first meeting with an enchantment. A somewhat wolf beast. At the start the ghostly friends ran darn hard after meeting the

Halflings, the twins would look at each other and leave their fur blanket over their shoulders to save some time for the entities to run and get away from the Halflings... The ghostly friends stood face to face with a half wolf and half humanly fantastic, they stared at each other, without anything happening... Later they became lovers in disguise.

Part 12

In the civilized world, the Halflings used to have wolf dogs with the same color eyes like theirs, turning the same color with every transformation or change… not alone wolf dogs, but many creatures from Dorthrin Firegale to take care of them and visa versa, and that they loved dearly with their whole heart including phoenixes… They loved their phoenix bird, wolf dog, and guns with silver and golden bullets in the best condition and never weakened them by constant training… Their wolf dog was their sweetheart and better ones have never crossed their way… two qualities that characterize a true top athlete are speed of mind and agility...

The thought of a life giving birth to more children… The twins lived in peace side by side with their ghostly friend and beastly enchantments, shrubberies and creatures for many years in both worlds…

There was a need of a rope and many power to pull a brave child hit by a pedophile up to accomplish the same bravery of a beast or creature like a wolf dog… or any animals nobility…

Although the pedophiles souls were swimming lively in the doomed world of hell, wholly nowhere to be found in the civilized world, only enlightened as an entity in the sea and wandering demons in hell, the enchanted noble four-legged wolf beasts stood still motionless… The Halflings and their ghostly friends wanted to lend the children a helping hand by carrying them and to release them from their faith… A crime convicted by another pedophile… what the twins would like to do for the kid!

The Halflings and their ghostly friends can't do and don't believe in magic, their minds are too enlightened for that and they've experienced too much in both worlds. But still, with that asshole of a demonic pedophile they were at the end of their rope! Once he hit a child victim so close to them they could almost have hit him with their gun…

Weight is worth gold! The entities in the sea were running wild according to the ladybirds and gentle-birds and needed to be tamed. So the Halflings climbed on their surfboard… They thought the entities to walk first at a walking pace, than at a briskly walk and finally at a trot… Then again, on the table of cocaine… Redoing the entire miniature, to the great amusement of those present, to the great surprise it was excellent without breaking a single cup or plate... they got to keep the surfboard as a gift, the entities were tamed at last...

The demonic entities stood stiff as a stick in battle formation, until they realized that their two winged Halfling twins originating from Dorthrin Firegale and planet earth, in both worlds, threatened to close into them with a little help, whereupon they struck with force!

Blacky! Your child... My child... With some help in the battle formation, they healed a child's wound magically well, something like that could only happen to this child! In encounter with the enemy the twins don't wish to claim any personal achievement. The success with which they brought this pedophilic and demonic enterprise to an end in the entire civilized world...

The giant from hell visited Superbia by invitation from the Halflings and had its innate courtesy, which made him beloved by rich and poor... But in these circumstances he neither had time to take off his shoes, nor did he find an opportunity to apologize for this audacity... However, his brave actions resulted in a minor inconvenience... He had gained nothing, unless it was his own life!

Blacky, the child and the twins were rescued by a passenger...

Blacky and the Halflings got stuck in sinking mud nearby the sea... How did they get out!

By being pulled by their hair and the child's soul by a friendly giant, and they got themselves out of the mud… This led to the invite.

The giant wasn't spared from misfortune. In a nightly adventure he was taken away as a prisoner in hell. His daily task wasn't hard. Everything shined like gold now…

Part 13

The demonic ghostly friends were hanging at least a few miles above the waters and in the middle of the clouds, numbed, they lay there. Hearts beating fast as if their heart was about to burst from the cocaine they where using on the plane. They racked their brains how to get out of the flight tomb. Finally they saw no other solution than to jump and think about going home…

With this they dived laboriously one-by-one towards the clouds. They succeeded in all this before the list noticed their temporarily absence… In the meantime the Halflings were in the presence of a creature, another bear, a demonic one that they had to offer to Hell. In order to attract the demonic bear they needed flaming honey… with the flaming honey they trapped the

demonic bear and they could offer
the bear to their grandfather *Lucifer*
in return for freedom!

The twins got their freedom. The
winter was very cold in the civilized
world. In their journey with the
giant to return to Superbia they
experienced greater discomfort than
on the journey to the civilized
world…

In Superbia, like *Popeye* the giant
had to carry the carriage in a small
road with an oncoming carriage on
the left side of the road to make
place for both to pass through…

The giant united the rides and
carried them with full strength
without effort and it was a
succession…

"God bless our great King and
Beauty Queen" their excellent
mother, L, and superior father, S,

laid honor, for quite some time with many words of wisdom...

There are adventurers that the Halflings and the giant surprisingly can't tell more than the urge to their actual experience. If there is any among you who doubt the giants true love of truth, then it must say that it sincerely regrets the lack of trust... the very first trip of the giant's life was over the sea... "Not yet dry behind the ears"

Part 14

A phoenix uncle from Dorthrin,
with great affection for the Halflings
did everything in his power to make
their wishes come true!

Shrubberies. Flowers and trees, with
roots coming out of the ground that
reach for the call in the clouds in
Superbia. For the two Halflings to
return…

A demonic forest giant killed
instantly!

At university in Dorthrin the
Halflings got on the throne. But the
twins remained behind in the
shadows of a swamp and for
summer break they finally sank
exhausted on earth.

To have a taste in hell during some
time abroad, a gigantic demonic lion
had fixed its eyes on the twins with

a look that showed a healthy appetite. Out of instinct they did what was left to do, run darn hard, they fled. They passed their time abroad with an A+.

Behind them stood a demonic lion from hell, in front of them a demonic crocodile, to their left was the mores and to their right a bricked abyss, in which demonic poisonous snakes swarmed... The Halflings fate, was either to be crushed or be torn apart.

Instead of their stipulated fate, the giant demonic lion ran into the mouth of the demonic crocodile! The crocodile ate the lion and they were saved by an unexplained noise coming out of the forest!

The demonic giant lion was killed and the big demonic crocodile too by such a huge meal. Their demonic friendly giant companion was soon at the spot and they threw themselves into each other's arms. Crying with joy… the skin of a crocodile was intruding. They occasionally add something of their own liking. How much this hurts and involves damage. The Halflings and their demonic ghostly friends live in a doubtfully world. Humans in the civilized world who don't know them are kept in custody with distrust and that hurts them to the core of their heart!

On their way back to the Dorthrin they traveled crossing England where they met the Queen and King of England

An Englishman, who with a whip clearly legibly cracked the two capital letters in the air of the Halflings parents' Royal names, sometimes with the crown still attached.

The demonic friendly giants own head was driven into its stomach area and it took years for the demonic giant's regular height, for it to regain original position from a sinking ship. Thanks to the demonic pelican, whose beak the Halflings handled to grab and to return unharmed on their way home...

The demonic friendly giant had a hole in his bucket with magical poison that it handled to cover with his bum! No need to take off its clothes. Those who think that this is impossible with such a cave should consider that the demonic friendly giant is of royalty!

Part 15

On one of the twins adventures back home to Dorthrin, The Halflings also experienced great danger in the Mediterranean flames too. These fires formed a border with Hell and the purgatory lands. A giant demonic fish ate them! It was pitch dark there, but also warm. They got an idea that by causing pain they would get out and be released...

Soon the demonic ghostly friends and the twins were greeted by an enchanted demonic Italian entity. He was close to death by suffocating. He died from a burst aorta when he laid his eyes on a naked demonic seductive woman from hell stepping straight towards him on the beaches of the sea. He couldn't possibly describe the amazement that was written in everyone's face on the naked beach…

One morning in the civilized world, while the Uriela and her ghost girlfriend were enjoying the beauty of themselves looking in the mirror, both saw high a spherical object about two meters in diameter in the sky, with something moving attached to it. They called upon Raphael and his ghost friend who were chilling with music and cocaine, playing a game of chess, and they held their heaviest gun… This time their first gun shot worked, all their bullets hit the cloth and tore the ball open on one side and it came falling down…

A very richly and glided barge with a *redrum* humanly man in it and a half roasted sheep fell into the sea water a few yards from them! They left their only creaturely servants to raw towards the air-traveling stranger. He was a Frenchman vampire and a sinner too…

"I'm a Frenchman and I took off about seven or six days ago. I can't tell exactly, because all that time I was at a height where the sun doesn't set anymore. I had lost all sense of time."

Hunger for heart tear gradually overcame the twin's scientific urges and instead of using the sheep for a study of blood and breathing, they slaughtered it on the second day and guzzled it up. Because the demonic vampire stranger thought he was somewhere else. "My long air balloon flight" he said. "Is due to the refusal of the cord that was supposed to let the gas escape. And if you hadn't shoot me down, I would have been suspended between heaven and earth until the

Day of Judgment, like the prophet Jesus Christ"… He was saved by the twins is what he thought.

Part 16

"My beasty heavenly friend, why
are you in such a hurry and why do
you carry such belongings?"

"I was in duty of a noble angel but I
got fired. I don't need my speed any
longer"

When it's not strictly necessary,
slowly hurry.

So L and S asked the angels if it
wanted to be of duty for them.

The next day they found a
wondering angel motionless in the
glooming clouds. "My angel friend,
what are you listening to?"

He was listening to the blooming
growing clouds.

"Well come into our service."

"You'll find that I appreciate such a gift."

And the angelic stood up on its two wings and followed S and L.

"My angel friend, great catch! But what have you been aiming on? We see a blue sky only."

The hunter replied that he shot an eagle bird on the towers of the gate. And he was right that the S and L instantly gave him a hug. Even this angel took part of their team.

The hunter angel bowed when it heard to take part of the crew belonging to the once well-known emperor wolf S and enchanted beauty L.

"Angel friend, what are you doing?"

"Madame and Sir, I need a smile, and since I've forgotten my fire I need to figure out how to help myself."

S and L would've rather offer their diamonds and gold than to let this angelic dude walk away without inviting it to their crew with a smile.

S and L where creating a fellowship consisting of 4 angels as companions for an adventure to planet earth to seek their children. They had untouched. Lost sight. Little did they know is that their twins were creating the same pack in hell bringing together the same souls but doomed in the fires of hell.

"My demonic friend, why are you in such a hurry and why do you carry such belongings?"

"I was in duty of a noble demon but I got fired. I don't need my speed any longer"

When it's not strictly necessary,
slowly hurry

So the Halflings asked the demon if
it wanted to be of duty for them.

The next day they found a
wondering demon motionless in the
glooming flames of grasses. "My
demonic friend, what are you
listening to?"

He was listening to the blooming
growing grass in flames.

"Well come into our service."

"You'll find that I appreciate such a
gift."

And the demonic entity stood up on
his two feet and followed the twins.

"My demonic friend, great catch!
But what have you been aiming on?

We see a clear landscape of hell only."

The hunter replied that it shot an eagle bird on the tower of Satan's entrance. And the entity was right that the twins instantly gave him a hug. Even this demon took part of their team.

The hunter bowed when it heard to take part of the crew belonging to the inherits of the once well-known emperor wolf S and enchanted beauty L. Without knowing that the same kind of group was being in formation in heaven to travel to earth.

"Demonic friend, what are you doing?"

"Uriela and Raphael, I need a smile, and since I've forgotten my fireballs I need to figure out how to help myself."

The Halflings would've rather offer their income inherited from their parents than to let this demonic fellow walk away without inviting him to their crew with a smile.

In the twins adventure with their demonic ghostly entities, with a team consisting of 4 new demonic friends, they passed the borders of Egypt and there was an overwhelming hurricane, that worried the twins for all of their demonic friends, including beasts, creatures and shrubberies and carriages to be blown away. There were windmills. Not far from the windmills stood a demonic man who held his left nose hole closed with a thumb blowing fire, and as soon as he saw the twins and their adventurous companions passing in uncomfortable condition he stood up on his legs and made a bow. It was if by magic! The fire stood still and had died with the windmills standing still. Also he took part of the team. He looked like the devil had entered his body or as if he was Satan himself in person. His skill was to make fireballs.

With one extra friend strong and an asset the Halflings and their demonic entity friends got on a yacht to travel over the sea.

Rough waters. The water seemed at first mirror smooth but later they could all save their lives by climbing trees like cats.

During their trip over the sea, they reached the other side of the sea in a land of wonders and reached *Aladin* within seven days. Satan himself, His Highness went so far in his goodwill that he allowed the traveling fellowship to choose as many demonic lovers as they pleased, making no exception for his own demonic favorites...

The Halflings have never troubled themselves with the stories of their adventures in hell and the purgatory world, and some they wishfully kept in silence as a secret about their voyages that have been traveled in that world in Dorthrin and civilization...

After their return from *Aladin*, *Satan* his paradise, the Halflings were his kingdoms light and sunshine. They could share the morning and evening glory. Consuming cocaine, and the most expensive drink? A Halfling knows what he's doing. Satan shared with the Halflings, their ghostly friends and demonic companions his cocaine, weed, precious and most expensive drink and poured his glass where after their glasses up until the top of the glass with liquor. They drank quietly and with attentive sips. The twins will always remember lines on the mirror table and the bottles that were branded with initials of their father, S, made by his co-soldiers, that was real cocaine! Satan received the cocaine from a man, who offered his own head…

Raphael made a bet with Satan that the cocaine they were consuming wasn't the best and that he could get better cocaine from a dear relation Maria. A bet. "If I don't keep my promise, then your majesty, you can have me beheaded and my head, is a small stake." If he'd succeed, then he'd receive as much gold and precious diamonds from his treasure as much as a strong man can rag out of it… *Avaritia* village would've been the following risk.

Uriela had a pen and paper and started writing to Maria.

"Maria! Your excellent cocaine. My brother and me want to ask you to send us 10 grams of cocaine, the one cocaine we've sniffed so often with you. Respectfully placing at the feet of your majesty with the assurance of our most intimate attachment, by having the honor to call upon ourselves"

A demonic messenger to the civilized world sent the letter.

As time passed Satan allowed the twins to view the garden in hell, but there were giant watchers that wouldn't leave them out of sight. That's how things stood, and the Halflings decided to invite their demonic friends. The sharpest listener and the best shooter. Their listener laid his ears on the ground once more and informed the twins that the messenger fell asleep because he could hear him snoring, albeit as a faint rumor. Once their shooter had heard of his job in advance he climbed into the highest porch and stood upon his toes. He saw a lazy demonic messenger, one lying at the foot of a shrubbery demonic oak tree. With the 10 gram of cocaine lying next to him. There was no need to worry. The demonic fellow would tickle him a bit with a bang!

The cocaine arrived safe and sound. Satan uncorked a bottle of *vodka* as a side dish and let the contents of cocaine slide down his throat with indescribable lust. "Giant, give my grandson and granddaughter as much gold and diamonds from my treasure room as much as the strongest man with a smile can carry. Hurry up!" The twins won the bet! It sounded like music in their ears!

The Halflings immediately sent their strongest demonic man with a smile...

Impatiently the twins hurried towards the harbor and bought a bigger yacht that was there for anchor. The engine was started in the blink of an eye. Little did they know that their worst fears were confirmed...

Once leaving the harbor they saw the entire demonic vampire navy commanded by Satan coming after them with full sail that it felt as their head was loose on their shoulder. But luckily they had their fireball blower on board. The speedboats were driven back, while in a few days they reached the coast of Italy...

In Italy, the twins and their ghostly friends had spend almost all their gold and diamonds to alms. On their way to Rome. Without a gesture of conscience. They took all that was left of the gold and diamonds, the thousandth part of their catch would've been enough for a full pardon to buy the *Voltorio*, leader of the vampires, up until the third generation…

The twins have the honor to wish you a pleasant sleep…

Part 17

After returning to private circumstances from running a business nearby the sea, readers from beyond were left overwhelmed with a cheerful mood. To reload, it didn't ask less than three hundred or thirty pounds, including the weight of a wedding ball that came along with a gun. S had to convince L that there was nothing to fear. Even a genie can look pale as death. A sample of unusual bravery...

Some people who need to be killed get protected and hidden. However, since the incident doesn't in the least detract from honor, S and L take the liberty of mentioning it in their absence. Not to entertain the slightest suspicion of their truthfulness. Should any of them have any mistrust in them, which they can hardly accept, let them know who they are…

The demonic ghostly friends were from a different cast with a same script. Their dads were born in a place where he was entrusted with the supervision of the cleanliness of the streets and squares. Their mother came from the mountains, an outgrowth of the neck. She left her parents at a young age and sought her fortune in the same city where their father first saw the light of day. This lovable duo met by chance on the street, when they were both drunk and bumped into each other at the same point. Here they saw their madness, reconciled with each other and got married. After their time was over their mother returned into her old profession but father, who had a highly developed sense of honor, left her for good…

The Halflings traveled to hell to greeting an old friendly giant friend who had acquired immortal laurels, which will never fade in eternity. And also informed the twins of the enemy's strengths...

The twins kept observing...

It was war...

Demonic enemy's sinking deeper and deeper into the sea by the mighty hand of the twin's artistic musical powers...

The demonic friendly giant welcomed the twins in Swahili "*Karibu*" and their visit was such a great success that he offered them a high position in his giant army. Instead, the Halflings were thankful and satisfied by the gesture of a dinner invitation that would remain indelible in their memories...

The demonic friendly giant disguises and protected the twins with every single visit, for they tolerated his presence until everything was discussed and then retired the rest... Because the Halflings got help with this it was the simplest job they have ever taken on...

The demonic friendly giant and the Halflings started a fire with the thought that no one would notice...

Demonic vampires fled to Paris within 14 days due to the fire. To live like a chameleons on air only. Satan, we'll put a bucket of brandy in front of their nose and they'll down it in one gulp...

In the battlefield in hell, a grenade fell in between the field of the enemy's camp. Taking a closer look with the demonic friendly giant's telescope there were demonic humans, sinners, on gallows kept hostage…

The twins threw a grenade…

Once they threw a grenade. Everything was ruined except for the two sinners alive that could release themselves from the gallows…

We spent the nights in such exuberant festivities with weed, liquor and cocaine that we had a hangover the next morning…

Another festive night…

Part 18

"What I'm telling you is nothing but naked truths! Passed down from father to daughter without interruption…"

There once was a hopeless red headed giant woman, who had not many years more left of her ripe, and had a choice according to her father but, no single man would fall for her charms and they would ran darn hard… "May I now be permitted to rescue from oblivion a few giants from that long line… A poet, who was also a reported poacher. His name was, I believe, *Shakespeare…*"

The hopeless giant, he thought he wanted to marry her… the poor Shakespeare was thrown to prison, but my giant ancestor nevertheless handled to free him in a very mad way… *Queen Elizabeth*, who ruled at that time, had gradually become so weary of life that the most insignificant actions cost her a lot of effort. Eating, drinking, dressing and undressing and other activities, that will be left unmentioned here, were all too much for her. She needed a replacement. The only reward he asked in return was to free *Shakespeare*. The affection for the famous writer was so deep that he would gladly have shortened his life to prolong the existence of his friend…

The Halflings and their demonic ghost friends lived as queens and kings of the underworld in the world of beautiful landscapes in the civilized world and Dorthrin Firegale… In the sea there lived monsters that lost their eyes, the demons ferocity disappeared and became as meek as a lamb… as a peculiarity, the twins didn't swim from A to B but walked, and indeed over the bottom of the sea. The speed, which it developed, was extraordinary, so that millions of demonic creatures moved in all directions away from their path. The demonic creatures also had something peculiar... there were some demonic creatures with large eyes as big as fruit scales and sometimes they would form a circle around the Halflings and sing the most complicated *Beethoven* song that the twins would play on their piano and guitar to increase their powers, and the demonic giants and creatures were stuck by their firmness of melody and purity in their voice.

The language of demonic creatures and demonic entities in the sea wasn't very known and the world underneath the sea started to notice that the Halflings and the ghost entities didn't belong... the situation began to be a bit tricky, as a demonic swordfish and demonic giant crab were pressing alarmingly close to them and a child's soul. Luckily the soul was blind. The child handled to reach the sea's beach by skillful maneuvering from the demonic pedophilic entity...

A giant was trying to figure out how stupidity works by landing himself in a big pile of hay in civilization... because he returned deaf to hell from this adventures he was blown into the sky and ended up into a haystack many miles away...

Part 19

In an adventure through the darkness of hell and the civilized world the twins succeeded to have a moment with personal beasty wolf friends of the twins. They traveled together in a demonic world and their prophecy were struck by an ice mass in the darkened mountains of hell. They saw a couple of demonic polar bears locked in a fight to the death. Later they figured out that the two demonic polar bears were just playing with each other. At the same moment the twins slipped and lost consciousness. The monsters had dragged them and they found themselves in a completely different world. They took their gun and killed. The shot was fatal. However, the shot woke other demonic bears from their sleep and they came towards them. They directly stripped the dead bears off their fur

and crawled in it as fast as lightning.
Their trick succeeded admirably.
The result seemed to satisfy them.
The mutual trust in the wolf pack
became even closer…

Their shrubbery tree friend once
said that a strong stab in the spine
causes instant death. If the
prediction hadn't come true, it
would've been over for them and a
fatal death, because the demonic
beasts would have torn them into
pieces, but fortunately it fell like a
block without moving a fin… Once
they saw them all lying dead
surrounding them they couldn't
suppress a certain feeling of pride…
They sent the furs to their beasty
wolf friends at home. In gratitude
they got invited to an annual dinner
and, to share the bed with the
bubbling passion of a wolf or
wolverine lover. As for their power
over the other sex they're puzzled,

because those lovers are certainly not the only one with affection and the twins belonged to their demonic ghostly relationships… The friendly relationship with their personal beasty wolf travel fellows deemed. The beasty wolf friends were consumed by jealousy. They were so jealous that he and she had fooled the monster animals by appearing in the middle with their head uncovered from the skin of the demonic bears they killed…

Some innocent and demonic humans and wolves take shit. There are shit flies that big, that some humans and beasts consume more shit than these shit flies, that even demonic humans themselves were frightened of these shit flies… The twins know that it doesn't make sense but they'd love to write about the affection they want to have with their future animal family members, a phoenix and wolf dog. Their phoenix and wolf dog stood there like a stick. This didn't shake their confidence in their wolf dog and phoenix for a moment. They declare that they have more confidence in their phoenix and wolf dog than all humanity and wolfs put together in both worlds. Life in hell and the purgatory world thought they were crazy by putting their wolf dog and phoenix first, even to the point of a bet. In the meantime, their phoenix hadn't moved a bit, which strengthened their conviction. The phoenix and wolf dogs found a vampire team up with a demonic pedophile committing a crime on a child at the age of 4 months…

The flight landed into the sea directly from a full moon by night into quiet waters… The Halflings visited hell earlier. Until halfway across the *seven sins* everything goes well and there is nothing remarkable to report home other than flying demonic women and men, who perform a graceful ballet…

A demonic three headed vulture commanded by a demonic workforce soldier is tremendously exceptional unless the human sinner or demonic vampire is sent by Satan from hell to seek more deaths… Hell was inhabited. When visiting the demonic friendly giant the Halflings saw great figures riding on big 4 headed vultures with a wingspan from one wingtip to the other as wide as the biggest demonic eagle on planet earth. Apparently in hell they are used as horses. Hell. In that world everything is gigantic. A mosquito there is as big as a sheep in the civilized world. The most used thing as a weapon is a flaming fireball, which they use as a defense and that armor is always deadly…to fight and keep the head intact takes a high price… In hell. When the fireball season is over, they use flaming fire arrows. Giant mushrooms are used as their shields. Then there are darkened immigrant souls that settle for temporarily for business. These demons have the faces of bulldogs and they wear their eyes on nostrils. Without eyelids, so that they can cover their eyes with their tongues to go to sleep. Their average height is 20 meters while among the habitants of hell none is under the 40 meters. Also the pleasure of love is unknown, because there is only one sex. Literally everything, demonic shrubbery, beasts and even demonic creatures, grow on flaming fires. Once they are ripe. When the *Beethoven* note has broken, a living animal emerges. So from one note comes a devilish dancer, from another a demonic philosopher, from the next a devils lawyer and from the fourth a malevolent doctor and everyone immediately begins to practice what they already know in theory...

Some lives in hells darkness chop of body parts but the cost of a losing head carries a much higher burden... To release a losing head sounds like freedom to those who chop the head that was intended to keep for eternal flames... For hell dwellers death is even easier, because they don't die. When their hour has come they dissolve into the air and disappear. The lives in hell don't drink. Certain dwellers lives in the darkness they have 1 finger on each hand, which they do more with than humans do with 5. They carry their head under their arm. It's also remarkable that the hell dwellers use their belly as their bag. They have no intestines, not even a heart. They don't wear clothes. They have peculiar eyes that are for sale on the market. If they lose or break an eye, they buy another. Current fashion in the darkness of hell changes quickly there and can go from green to blue eyes in a day...

Part 20

The party the Halflings attended
were always hammering and full of
sex, drugs and rock and roll...
Something only imaginable and to
be present in dreams... They make
peace and hate fights and wars that
they don't want to create nor take
part in anymore... They still look
fresh, among fabulous demonic
humans, and reading seems to affect
you more than my words... This
adorable attention gives the twins
the courage to finally treat you to
almost some unbelievable
adventures of which the authenticity
their parents nevertheless wish to
personally guarantee...

"They are so beautiful, clever and
kind..." said their parents.

The flight. The demonic ghost
entities were in custody with a

desire to see Lucifer themselves. Determined to penetrate into the bowels of this volcano, even if they'd risked their life. With unheard-of determination they reached the top and looked with horror into the boiling funnel. Suddenly they made up their mind to let themselves fall. Because they fell faster than the glooming coals flew against them, they nevertheless reached the bottom alive... And who did they meet? It was Lucifer in person. His surprising appearance, however, restored peace and the demonic ghost friends generously exchanged their hands with that of Lucifer. He had the goodness to bind up their wounds with plasters with his own hands that healed immediately...

The demonic ghost friends found a true beauty queen watching herself in front of the mirror that they greeted kneeling in the eyes of Lucifer while she was preparing herself in-front of the mirror, like a real gentleman towards a beautiful lady… He introduced his divine Medusa to them and urged her to oblige them in everything. Perceiving from the trembling in their voice this was a matter that had to unfortunately be refrained from describing the softness of her voice and the luxury of her affection… The ghosts could never guess that Uriela and Raphael were family of both, Lucifer and the hell goddess.

The ghost entities have learned a lot from such informative conversations with Lucifer and Medusa. If Satan's evil tongue hadn't whispered something about them in the ear of her husband. Without the least ceremony, one morning, when they were attending his wife's toilet, he held the entities by the collar and led them into a chamber, which they never entered before. And Satan said: "Ungrateful immortals! Return to the world from which you came! As an entity in ghostly skeleton form and thou shall be friends with twins and mislead them into desire without affection and bring them to me" And without giving the ghostly boy and girl the chance to say anything in their defense, he let the boy and girls skeleton fall headlong into the ground… into the water, out of the plane tomb, and let their soul swim to the shore…

Who knew that an afternoon windsurfing in restful waters with minimal waves with a wind bringing the twins to new demonic friends, a new adventure into a new world with a few demonic humans

swimming close to the shore
without noticing the demonic
entities of the sea... Who knows
what he or she has to bring to the
table the twins wondered... Then
demonic ghost entities began to feel
dizzy and lost consciousness. But at
last they came to their senses by
reeling themselves immersed in
water that became clearer and
clearer by the rising sunlight until,
they came into the surface, they saw
themselves surrounded by its
radiant light. Now the entities could
swim excellently and, compared
with what they had just gone
through, it felt as if they were in
paradise... They saw nothing but
water.

Dawn was beginning to fall when
one of the Halflings suddenly
spotted a wracked flight sinking and
headed straight for it on their
surfing boards. The demonic ghost

friends saw one of the twins coming and jelled at them with all their might, within range of calling, and received an answer in Latin. They told the Halflings that they were divines from the Sea and that they were wondering souls in between two worlds just like them, and with that being said the situation was immediately clear to the twins. The demonic ghost friends had fallen right through the center of the earth to the other side, which is a considerably shorter route than the usual trip around the world… Rude people those sinners. The Captain of the flight didn't make it and was the greatest sinner. This, because he told lies as if it was completely truest. Because the demonic ghost entities, now lovers of the Halflings owed their life to their saving, sent by Satan with the duty to gratitude and to tolerate the insult without punishment to hell. When the ghosts got invited onto the twins yacht they asked about their next destination, they got the answer that the twins were making an *rendezvous*, a voyage of discovery on the sea worlds…

Traveling over the sea from one world to another world brought heavy and bumpy and rough storms alongside the journey… A terrible storm arose that tore all the engines of the yacht into pieces. The place where their compass was, was completely shattered. Every sailor knows what the consequences are. At last, the storm began to calm down and changed into a strong breeze. A strange, unknown bliss filled the Halflings minds and they inhaled in amazement the mist fragrant perfumes. Even the sea lost its green color and looked *Bordeaux red*…

The demonic ghosts friends got unconscious from the adventure and the thing that they had discovered… Despicable twins… They swept the demonic ghosts of their feet… The Halflings explored a new island on the sea and it even had a harbor, which seemed surprisingly big to them. It turned out to be filled not with water, but with full-fat crystal clear blood. Here they moored at a darkened island, which consisted of one enormous piece of skeletons. Apparently the demonic ghost friend on board, had an invincible aversion to skeletons, she politely but urgently requested the Halflings to remove that wretched skeleton from under her feet. She was right, the messengers of this island where nothing but skeletons.

The discovery brought them to four legged demonic goats as well… they were fast… on this island they also found a large quantity of vineyards, with the grapes that appeared to contain crystal clear blood only. The demons. They had 4 legs and only 1 arm and, when adults, they wear a horn on their foreheads, which they made very clever, use of. Deeper inlands we discovered 7 more rivers with blood and 2 with liquids of *Gin Tonic.* After 16 days of walking they reached the coast on the other side and here the ground consisted of white, very mature cocaine.

In this island, a world of demonic baby owl bird animals are being haunted by demonic animals… they are each other's enemies instead of friends… the demonic baby isn't even fully awaken and the egg shell is being opened by demonic kindred spirits to kill the demonic baby animal… in the Crowns of the 4 legged creatures nested gigantic owl birds. So the Halflings and their ghost friends found a nest. About 1 million eggs and the smallest of them had the contents of a huge barrel of beer. With difficulty, the Halflings handled to lift out the largest egg and smash it. A naked demonic owl chick, 10 times the size of a full-grown demonic vulture, came out!

They eventually landed on property of the island that was lived by demonic beastly, devilish creaturely and shrubbery, that in turn were being fed by kindred spirits to grow… it was an desert island were beasts, creatures and shrubberies of same spirits didn't live side by side but were each other's enemies… The demonic mother bird fell down and came to rescue with outspread claws and held the flight's Captain to release him once more into the sea among other entities. Now demonic entities swim like rats and after a while they were harmed back into hell. On the way back to Superbia the Halflings killed two more buffaloes, which had only 1 horn and that right between the eyes. Their meat tasted excellent, although the inhabitants of hell themselves, who lived only on crystal clear blood and cocaine, had an aversion to it… Up to their discovery, the island belonged to the purgatory world, a village named *Gula* they discovered.

The twins wonder if someone who tells only lies, he or she deserves punishment, the first duty is to stick to the truth. Back on the yacht with engines prepared by the boys they weighed anchor and the Halflings and their ghostly companions sailed away from this land of worth. All the shrubbery trees along the coast in Gula bowed very deeply and exactly the same, wishing the Halflings farewell.

During the journey over the sea the twins and their friends saw a big fish crossing their way towards the yacht that was twice the size of their *Holterman* yacht... After some days they arrived, hell knows where, for they had no compass, into almost pitch-black darkened water. They found to their unspeakable surprise that it was pure and unmixed blood! The Halflings, had to restrain themselves from drinking themselves into a stupor! A few hours later they found themselves surrounded by gigantic demonic whales. One of these evil monsters swam quietly nearby opened its mouth and swallowed the whole yacht with ease as if it were an XTC-pill. Carried along by the water, their yacht entered its stomach. The atmosphere inside, however, was very cold and humid. The amount of water the monster swallowed was almost equal to the lake of *Genève in Switzerland* as viewed in the civilized world…

Between hell and Gula on their way to Superbia, they caught a gigantic demonic whale on their way, and as both Sagittarius with their bow… He was never satisfied and never full… The demonic ghost friends elected both Halflings as chairmen and they immediately brought up the idea of placing both their bow when the demonic monster spreads its baldhead. Their ghost friends adopted this motion unanimously. And what seemed, the demonic animal opened its mouth and they could immediately ram the bow between its tongue and appetite so that it couldn't close its mouth. As soon as they were back in the open sea they could enjoy the beneficial sunlight that they have been deprived of for nearly 6 months! Gradually all victims floated out of the whale and finally they found themselves with 75 nationalities. They left the bow exactly where it was to save others from the same misfortune...

Towards Superbia the Halflings and their friends met Teddy the demonic friendly bear who greeted them with great pleasure and he growled at them as if he expected their visit... All but all it was a pleasure to meet Teddy the demonic friendly bear who their demonic ghostly friends have had for many years on their night stand but appeared as a real lively bear, before their curse, they kept Teddy as a puppet, but this time it was all jazz and lively... They traveled in good spirit to Superbia, and the twins were the first to set foot on land. Dorthrin. Here an enlightened demonic beastly bear greets them. Without hesitation they held both its claws and shook them so heartily that the enchanted animal began to weep with emotion, they weren't dismayed, and continued shaking it until it died of sheer magical emotion. This event insured such a sacred respect by the other captivated bears that the twins and their fellowships have never met one since...

To be aware of their imprinted dreams of father S and mother L, for them to take over their nightshifts when both the Halflings are asleep, their animal, shrubbery and beastly uncles and aunties bought wolf dogs for them, each with one... not a regular wolf dog but a gigantic wolf dog... A wolf dog to protect them from harm... Back in Dorthrin they were delighted by their old beasty wolf friends they met there with a gift. This turned out to be a hunting phoenix... Which was still descended from the famous bitch they already met during their growth and that had given birth to her youngsters during their great discovery. Unfortunately, the mother phoenix was later fatally shot by a clumsy vampire hunter. However, the feathers were made into a pen that was also used by their mother L to write to their father S, the emperor wolf. This feather pen has the property of infallibly leading them to a palace where a wild chess game is…

As you can read I, S, have only a few time left, but let me add some new ones. Whoever of you visits us won't have anything to complain about. Now however, will you allow us to go to bed and wish you all a sweet dream and a good night…

The Halflings woke up from a
fantastic unconditional dream full of
secrets beyond adventures from one
place of the world to another with
the love sent from hell and heaven
imprinted in their dreams...

Part 21

Uriela is a grown schoolgirl too and decided to stay like this for the rest of her life that turned to be in contact through the Sea with her demonic ghostly entity that was a gold digger who is rich and a millionaire. The ghostly friend wasn't hat friendly. A vampire demon that was sent by Satan that mislead their parents during their wedding also sent demons, demonic ghostly malevolent friends to let the twins fall head over heals with them and sign Satan's contract. Clumsy and foolish Uriela and Raphael. They eventually fell for the charms of the demonic ghostly girl and boyfriend because of their generosity, craziness, charms and looks. Up to a surprise, the demonic ghost friends grew towards loving them and were also into their beastly heart. After experimenting with drugs and playing water sports the twins they grew stronger feelings towards their betraying entities who had no golden time that lasted and were slowly fading. Under pressure of Satan's eyes. Whith Satan not knowing that they were dating at a sudden moment in life. Uriela suggests spending a while in Dorthrin where her brother Raphael is doing business with the Giants because, something was on the rise and Uriela and Raphael couldn't have a 'normal' relationship together. It was better for them to leave their relation for what it was. It was as if something came between their bond. Little did the prophecy know that the twins their relation and the bond they have between them is so strong that something beautiful and enchanted bloomed out of their relation after their first kiss! But before Uriela and Raphael and their demonic ghost friends continue the relationship in a more formal form the demonic ghost friends betray them with a contract that he and she want the twins to sign with conditions to continue their relation. The contract consisted of a long-lasting imprint of their memories after fading away and in smaller letters a deal in hells darkness under the ruler of Satan's power. Before the ring or signing any contract both twins decide to go for a break to Dorthrin to meet their raisers to let them read the deadly contract that their new demonic friends propelled to them. After their stay in Dorthrin, the entire situation between the twins and their ghostly friends was a game and the twins dreamed once more…

There was a precursor that Uriela was about to lose her virginity from her imprint with the devil. Satan had his eyes on her since she was born. The devil, Satan, looked at her nodding. He captured her in her dream and held her under vision. It felt like being handcuffed by a bad cup and she couldn't make a move. She was held hostage in the darkness of hell under Satan's flaming eyes, he showed up tall with great posture and a deep voice. She estimated his appearance in her dreams as a figure in his early twenties. Satan can become visible in all forms especially into your strongest desire once held arrest under the eyes of a deadly contract. Her heart started pounding once he stood in front of her.

"Don't pretend to be so innocent my beauty darling" he says.

"You know exactly why you have to stay and may not pass."

She felt a blush on her cheeks because she thought he didn't notice, the boy of her fantasy, her demonic ghostly friend. She woke up wet and horny in her dreams and she decided to be naughty in her vision and take out her naughtiest masterpieces of clothing's out of her closet and wear her boots in her hallucination. The reason why she was wearing that masterpiece of clothing in her dream, the action of opening her blouse a little more and showing off her tits and boobs was not her intend. Including stockings with no tong and, yes, Satan made her do it on purpose. Satan deceived her by making her legs open a bit widely. Without looking at Satan. She even neglected eye-to-eye contact, so he would notice what her intentions were. It's was Satan's dirty fantasy and she pleasured herself that night with visions about her with Satan. But he caught her. Oops! He bended himself over her. He smelled her female odor.

"You are a clever picturesque girl, but also a naughty one." He whispered in her sleep.

"You have mislead me for a split moment in severe passing attempts and think I wouldn't notice your intentions in my darkened world, so tempting whilst you stood in front of my gate with your brother and your friends."

"Look at me" he says sighing in her dreams.

"Did you wear those masterpiece clothing's with those stockings for me or for that brother of yours you kissed. Is this why you doubt signing the contract that will lead you to me?" Satan questions self-doubting.

"For you!" she talked back in her sleep with confidence.

He grabbed her with his hands and lifted her up on his malevolent flaming desk. He himself sits himself in front of her on his master chair exploring her vagina. His hands glided on her knees targeted towards above while she opened her legs a little further in commandments. She felt his fingertips on her clit and fingering her g-spot.

"You are drenched" he whispered.

Then he started finger-fucking roughly, but unwelcoming. She moaned but Satan pulled his finger out. She begged him in her dreams from desire,

"Please me, fuck me…", while she laid herself almighty down on his desk and closed her eyes in her hallucination.

She heard how his zipper of his pants unzipped…

Satan deceived her like *the devils advocate*.

The demonic ghostly friend. He had a crush on Uriela. He knew about Satan's action and he was devastated. He truest had a crush on her. He was a demonic ghostly boyfriend that couldn't bind himself to a divine girl who finally concluded that he couldn't live without her. With the introduction of how he wanted her. Not that it's only going to be about intimacy, but the thought that he can't give himself fully without the thought of Satan's first touch on the virginity that she lost, to a girl he had feelings for with the realization that a crush like her could give herself fully to a man without marrying. Not knowing that Satan, the devil, mislead her through hallucinations and imprinted her thoughts and made Uriela believe it was him. It's not only about having confidence that is favorable it's also about the hollow by Satan and his game that has made the demonic boyfriend this way. To stick to Satan's plan. Break the twins.

After Dorthrin she decided to accept the contract with her ghost boyfriend from the Sea and made the call. But she wished that he would be more openly about his emotions. This might sound awkward, but seemed quite regular for a girl who accepted a boy in her

life and dreams, and for him to bond
more in a relationship. Both will
have moments of talks.
Communication combined with
some classic trauma and some
intimacy that lead to their first
clumsy kiss.

Uriela gifted her demonic gold
digging ghost friend in return by
surprising him with expensive gifts
straight once arrived at the Sea and
more trips with the helicopter over
the Sea and elsewhere from
Superbia to Invidia. Her ghost friend
is an impressively generous and rich
boy.

Up to one night after her dream. It
was raining roughly when Uriela
was chilling with her demonic ghost
friend's at her parents house that
both twins happened to not mind

for him staying over. They both liked each other and started to be more than just lovers. She suggested her ghost friend he'd stay over at her place near the Sea. The weather near the Sea was rusty and code red. Bedtime. Her ghostly boyfriend gave her a hug to show some affection with his great muscles and she gave him a kiss on his cheeks. She liked him back, but both didn't know how to even express their love and affection. The flames of fire turned into green. He had fallen for her. Her male ghost friend had great dick and beautiful body. She wondered how it would be if he would've put his manly hood in her mouth. He left the living room and left her to go to bed on her own pace. She started playing music on the piano. He headed to the shower. She wanted to know what he was up to after the shower. So she left the living room and headed to the bedroom to see his reflection on the wall in the darkened bedroom with a shimmering light while he was showering and she was waiting for him, naked on the twin-size bed. Waiting for him to get out of the shower. Once he was done showering she grabbed him by his butt and pulled his manly hood into her mouth. Her demonic ghost friend pushed her on the bed and turned her on her belly and he spit on his dick. He gently forced his manly hood in her. She started playing with herself by pushing her fingers on her fragile spot and started playing with herself while listening to the sound of him moaning…

It's a date. No rules and no secrets. Uriela is going out for dinner. It's a romantic date with his demonic boyfriend. They renegotiate the contract of Satan. Both yearn for each other more than Satan his thirst for sex that shall fade once the demonic ghostly entity shall diminish along the way over some time. Unconditional love conquers it all. No secrets about fakes, jealous ex's or disturbing creeps.

Some dramatic bumps for a good end. A handful good jokes from the Halflings towards their lovers. In the meanwhile there are less emotions to be read from the Halflings their faces. Their hopeless love turns into reprisal. The jalousie from the civilized crowd and the flaming eyes from dooming hell seen in their lovers causes stained eyes forsaking their lovers in fake signed contracts and a rise into the 7 sins from Dorthrin.

In the bedroom too, too many
excitement. It is all dreadfully much
heavier since the contract. The smart
Raphael, businessman and she,
Uriela made sure of a water closed
contract by the Sea before placing
their magnificent signature. Much
more than the gloom there is further
more to tell. Neglecting on a few
touching and a few handcuffs in
bed, the entire sex excitement hasn't
disappeared.

"I want you, and I can give you
what you want!" both twins moaned
in their lovers ears.

Part 22

Similar as for both, the twins have a purpose and dream in art and walk the same path as their mother and father's career. Raphael likewise as him, S, walks the path as an assigned guitarist in a rock band to make his destiny and dream come true and L, the twins mother, her daughter Uriela, she trained her proficiency as a piano player playing a symphony in a ballet piece as a pianist. Both convinced to make their parents dreams come true in the civilized world and Dorthrin. So is the game of chess S and L play before their sex routine. The twins play the game too but more in the fashion from Dorthrin with their beastly friends, wolves. The wolves and the twins love to play their games. Especially with the vamps, pedophiles and demonic entities as their pray. In quite some time, the game of chess became an innocent and famous crime in the media. If the twins and their wolf friends convicted a crime they played against the laws and chose their own crime in an convenient way. They killed their enemies in an selected way. After long nights, spilled with blood, the skies turned pink and blue. Pink if Uriela won the chess game and blue if it was Raphael his turn. What a difference the destiny of the enemies death could make. Later, the twins realized they committed a crime. Their parents could've look away the sins in heaven. They kept their criminal path as a secret in Dorthrin. In the civilized world they killed and were accused for something by someone that was a fanboy. The twins shot the enemies in an obvious way. It was all making sense. The Halflings, they play their addictive chess game on a glooming white and black board from the darkness in Dorthrin to attack in the civilized world to protect children from harm. With the game the chess pieces were divided into two groups, Dorthrin and hell. Decisions had to be made by game if the dead soul would get a penalty in the purgatory world of Dorthrin or be sent directly to the more darkened world in hell. The catch would result as habitants of these two worlds. The game was lead by giants and has been played during day and night. At night the wolves would cry for the forsaken moon and seek for bloody heart tear. During daylight the lives of children would be protected. An understandable artistic pursuit.

In heaven two lovers think for hours creating anxiety and romance during their game of cards and chess. Without overlooking in someone's head which romantic step they set on the scene and which rule encounters for the lover.

L and S, as young lovers in heaven they participated in the heavenly game of chess. With them everything is fine, but with their children nothing was going great. Their parents decided to move their darn ass out of heaven and to seek for their lovingly children. It was time and they had to come up with something against the Lord to leave the heavenly gates to appear has angels in the civilized world to defend a crime planned by their children. Their children were being mislead and sabotaged by an idiotic someone they could not oversee in heaven that was the leader of hells darkness. L and S had to come up with an excuse to defend their children's criminal minds before it was to late. Sometimes in paradise would play the game of chess when one of them was far away asleep. When you play the game without a partner the game would immediately start with L or S, depending who's having a beauty sleep, and would get started against someone else within a match against other heavenly angels. But this time without romantic rules. Except for S and L, which are heavenly partners. If L and S play, they would play the game with passionate verdicts that where given from their past life, with a touch here and a touch there, a kiss here and there a kiss once in a while after a movement. "First we must play against each other, after we play with our soulmates", S whispers in L's ears. Every chess game won by them resulted in harmony in heaven and in the civilized world. Birds would start to sing in spring. Trees would grow their leaves after a cold moment. Animals would start to lovingly bond in the hot summer. In the winter the creatures would gather enough food to stock and overwinter the time until it would be spring.

The realization kicks in fast how detail oriented the game is. Than it comes in hand. To be a chess lover. Within chess it has been a fad to gather mistakes of how the game is being played. Within the most common mistakes that exist in the game consisted of, chessboards that are arranged wrongly, pieces that are misplaced and personages that don't know how to move the pieces in chess. To avoid such elementary mistakes, chess players in heaven call upon the Lord *Jesus* or any prophecy of their religion as one of the best that tells about their religion in heaven how to play. The Lord.

He, has learnt many how chess must be played and how the pieces must be hit from the board.

There is no reduced amount of *Pico Bello's* and children of the *millenniums*. From a friends imprint S and L had to oversee the treatment of their Halflings and the growth of them from a distant. Until them growing into enchanting beasts and successful business divines on earth. Not knowing that their future would change path. They prayed for their twins they wouldn't convict a perfect crime. They were concerned the twins could kill innocent humans and neglect the rules for sending souls to hell's darkness. Although both hell worlds wasn't their parents territory. They were worried like every single parent would be from a distant.

The spaces in heaven that are organized for chess games are heavenly. But the strongest choices are made during chess games in darkened hell. With a little dose of cocaine that is being given for those with anxiety in the regime to stay in heaven, within this way the children in heaven would remain calm, and wouldn't be milked out for being melodramatic about it. Basically like none potential drama is being milked out, the plan doesn't chose for the chosen road. Medusa seemed to be a talented pianist but the system in hell diminishes that she could put a footstep outside of the doors of dooming hell to build a career in the civilized world or visa versa. Behind how many doors lay dead dreams?

Then twins and their parents', were thankful to play the game of chess, a strong mixture of oneself and they were introverted. L, she clearly has problems with bonding with angels, logically seen her background, but when it comes to chess, she doesn't let anything come all the way through. Especially not by man like the pedophile who raped her. He was playing her against the law, but she didn't have a clue. He got killed after all, the night before he put his dick into her. It was an awful kill committed by her husband. Both look back on it and loved it, except things started to make sense after that death. Such man needed to be vanished and rot in hell's flames. The luck that lovingly angels surround her, she has. Once L was off the cocaine, the rise of all those angels who think about her and who were concerned about her wellbeing

were there for her. The hidden
angels that care about L and love her
unconditionally.

Part 23

Horror and dreadfulness of the sound the twins made on their guitar and piano. The dark side of their success. Both their obsessive kindness of loyalty to a dark tone in their music that longs for playing white and black piano keys, balck an white guitar and black and white chess boards. The thirst for demons hearts tear. Their obsession for such led to *Der Untergang* of both of them in Dorthrin and severe lands, their talent and their paranoid search for the key of their parents death and each others love to research the universe until both fall for each others unconditional love by madness. The overdoses of drugs caused a one-time premature end. The contract with Satan was signed in twofold. Making them focus on the ultimate obsession, the overpower of the dead. Back on earth where the fights with the demons were countless, their bodies were being all set for the champion prize, until both in the last magical movement fell for the fading way, hell's darkness.

In reality, the Halflings had to train for the season opening of an orchestra if they chose to be in the famous world of howling demons in the masterpiece of *"fur Elise"*, and they played a majestic role in the music work of genius. Thoughts of their parents who weren't alive. The music their twins played was vulnerable and whispering spells that demons could feel. Uriela and Raphael officially received a beautiful role that suited them as vulnerable Halflings on their path to hell, both received the perfect role for the white and black beast like the piano keys on board of Satan's song of classic... But do both control the black and white beast in them, by their devilish extremes? There is a need of passion. The Halflings warn Satan and the laughing demons and its workforces. Technique is not enough. In a biggest, rawest silver lining work the Halflings go through a discovery of their devilish side to find it in their parents previous life. The Halflings must be and shall become the black and white piano keys, emperor beasts from hell, above Satan, ruler of all. Both discover that the lining between passion and sanity sometimes is thin as paper. It is a twilight zone where dramatic events take place.

The Halflings obsession becomes more real and visible. Both slowly develop a bipolarity. They envision sounds going louder and softer exactly during their spells spoken out to kill vampires they are longing to hear from lyrical music on their devises during musical instrument practices in the echo halls through their speakers. Or when both travel around the church realizing that driving circles and always reaching the same destination is that of the airport towards their escape where both got into. Both also got into a plane of what both thought it went to the destination above "The Sea" towards their hometown but eventually figured out that they stepped into the wrong airplane. Both planes back home left on a different platform than usual. Both thoughts where focused on the *sound of music*. So seductive. Once both figured out that the airplane wasn't going home both got out at a place where both didn't trusted the taxi driver that was option two both once called to bring them back home towards the Sea. Option one was to surf back home over demonic entities and demonic creatures lives of the waters that was a no go. The last option both figured was to call the police in the hope both would be brought back home. The madness of the pianist and guitarist was one big cliché, just like the many other creative sufferings of most artists like *van Gogh*.

Because of their bipolar every breath and every single movement of their guitar and piano tones were hearable what caused a breakable, and oppressive thinking. Just like the creepy and suffocating thought of their mother who saw her own piano career fail, and now the

Halflings delusion suggest that their mother is trying to sabotage their deal with Satan, although both their grandfather and grandmother, Lucifer and Medusa, wanted them to rest because they knew and realized that the twins were sick. The Halflings original mother, L her imprint towards the twins started to slip away while she felt the need to protect them. The Halflings had hallucinations that came along with their bipolar. Their hallucinations consisted of biting nails up until their bones because they admire meat beside their strictly diet, street lights that burned together, scratching skin that caused rashes that didn't want to disappear on the under legs. Their crisis situation is that both live from their diet tans like a Jew in world war 2. Their transformation from blood to flesh mirrors the change of their soul.

The Halflings their will to win in hell and their fear to lose are their most destructive powers. Both no longer work towards the Dorthrin dream, but crashed in the devilish madness in the deepest fires of hell, in a grimy universe wherein everyone seems to be busy with themselves. But is it really so? It is to cliché to judge that for success we do the most terrible things to one another, especially when it consists of desirable fame. The Halflings ghostly friends try to break them and to ruin their world, but it is never clear if it is a slither deal from hell or whether it is their suspicion… Reality and nightmare becomes more inseparable when the perspective of the Halflings stress, exhaustion and blind ambition looks twisted.

The more the Halflings look on the world and the reality in life everything seems to come closely together, the more they evolve into both the black and the white devilish beasts similar to the "*Listz*". The adventurous show begins. It makes the devilish beasts a grandiose derailing symphony. The Halflings metamorphose is complete. The orchestral piano music swells until the moment where everything crescendo comes together in the final transformation above Satan, the biggest movement in the finale sight, the apotheoses where art and life coalesce.

Both were guitarists and pianists that gained and aspired a majestic role in "*Beethoven*" and were a pray to madness by their bipolar and suicide attempt out of loving and missing their parents horrifically. The piano and guitar is a sport where body and soul are being demolished. The Halflings rose above themselves as a devilish beasts king and queen in hell.

The Halflings find out that their mother happened to be a ballerina. L, started dancing when she was a child, but couldn't reach the highest stage unless she embraced her sexuality. Uriela, slept in her home for a long time that was her child room and slept between Ted's the fake bears on her night stand. Uriela attended the same piano classes like her mother and the piano teacher screamed the symphony and that she is frigid, although the prudish took advantage of this by going out one evening clubbing to experiment with drugs and kissing with a girl what lead to her feelings for girls and became bisexual when she was eight.

The love for girls and boys can't be muffled away, the ambitious Uriela that feared penetration from childhood to adolescence, and through her work of art became urged to lose her virginity. It may be clear that blood shall pour. The escalation of delusions and self-mutilation feeds her to a taste of her own blood from an open wound that both, for Uriela and Raphael, causes the change into the devilish beasts of hell as the spectator works liberating.

The deeper demons sank, the higher the children of L and S could rise.

The Halflings became famous guitarists and pianists in the darkness that gave their everything to make the madness flagrant. In their sickness playing the guitar and piano they passed the dream with their dreadfulness guitar and piano in eternal fires of hell with their generous friends that turned into demonic lovers. Who hope to react unprecedented heights as rock and classic starting points and want to be launched like a star.

Part 24

In a moment it became winter.
Almost the entire summer the
fading ghosts spent time with the
Halflings. The golden time to change
and dissolve. Before the Halflings
and the demonic ghostly friends had
spent time together at the old tower
in Dorthrin without guidance
nearby the Dandelions field airborne
as if it where their own kingdom.
They over thought to leave their
homes behind and to buy a house in
hell, because the Halflings couldn't
imagine themselves growing old
together in the homes they inherited
there, and all four felt bashful. If all
went to the home, it would only be
to check if both Halflings got mail
from creatures, shrubberies and
beasts from Dorthrin. Until now it
was just an option, both didn't make
a definite decision, but slowly all
started to pack things and putting

stuff in boxes all arranged and prearranged accordingly in masterpieces with labeling boxes, while cutting and moaning the lawn and flowering the roses of their new land house. Black roses.

A letter from mother…

Once upon a midnight diary wherein I write to you my beloved children… I said farewell to the world, but your father didn't believe that I meant it this time. He left his lips on a sensual way like he usually does, and I listened to blistering whispers in my ear from him. This time his promises were no longer enough for me. He looked at me confirming that he uses pleasure as a façade to reveal his love. Deep in his dark brown eyes, I saw something glooming of love, I knew I was right,

*that there is more to him than what he
shows. But I'm not blind anymore. I
know now that I'm the woman that can
reveal the man behind the Mastermind.
I will take part of his journey, and he of
mine.*

*A part of me hopes that he will miss me
when we part, that we shall appraise
each other the way we are one day. Both
as a divine. I didn't dare to under see
him in his eyes and to touch him out of
fear that he'll weaken in the thought of
the change. I have a handwritten note
that I left on your desk, wherein I tell
everything what I have to say about our
last trip. We should be back by Friday
and if we don't. I love you. Always and
forever. With every breath you take, I'll
be here for you.*

"Goodbye. With love. L" Your mother."

Mother has left the Halflings with a new discovery and they only have a few moments in time before the change to live in hells darkness. They are prepared to take risks with knowing about the secrets they keep between them about their parent's death and where they belong.

L awakens and hears the voice of S, and looks how he looks up to her, she rises out of bed, afraid that she is dreaming. S lets her know to hope that there is still a chance for them as parents. He gets on his knees, but doesn't touch L. A terrible feeling makes him a master of cards.

S tells L if she wants to know exactly how their son and daughter are doing, she'll have to find this out in a spirit to planet earth. Their imprints aren't able to be fussy or chased neither from Dorthrin's messenger nor on earth. S secretly has report from his phoenix that will be meeting and welcoming them when they will arrive at destination. She always knew, but she was never ready for it. She's not sure if she ever will be ready for the vision of the lost bond between her twins. Therefore L will have to wake up tomorrow in heaven and think about it long and thoroughly enough if she wants to dream.

'Our Passports…' she speaks as a secure queen from heaven.

He digs in his inside pocket and confirms he has them. She hasn't touched me still, S wonders.

Why doesn't she touch me? This is too sudden. My eyes in my skull spin.

'Please, lets talk about this.'

'No, I don't want to talk. No way! Everything or nothing, S.'

'This is my offer, and you have to decide if you really want this. There lays a one-way-ticket with your name at the airport. With a flight over "The Sea" I'm in the previous airplane. I really hope to see you there.' L says.

She walks away and closes the gate behind her. She has disappeared and leaves S behind with the proof what she's tasted from him earlier, there is more behind this flight than she knows, and there are more unconditional secrets beyond love to be revealed.

Part 25

It happened! Revenge. The Halflings strike on earth and over the lands in the purgatory, to hunt for human souls and those of precious and beloved shrubberies, creatures and animals. Sending demons and Satan's servants to do the filthy job for them in Superbia and other villages counting the hunt on innocent souls, without mercy and without making their hands dirty.

In the civilized world. It all happens at the dawn of the night. In Dorthrin they hit when the flames of hell are on its lowest. Tricky. The twins revealed this secret to Satan that gave Satan's servants and watchers great catches of the most beloved beasts and shrubberies. On planet earth. At night they sent demons to knock and ring at humans doors on the 13th of the month. Every thirteenth of the night. They command their innocent souls to go out and party with them and drugged them with blood poison to become new born in the flames of the deepest fires of hell. After this night the innocent human souls wouldn't deal with daylight and this was their last night as a human, in eternal darkness belonging to the Nosfuratu's. When humans live alone with or without their wives and children, they chase at night on specific times and even one moment few souls couldn't remember that it would be their last night that their spirit would remain in darkness, and it would be its last night as a civilian. The Halflings had a darkness formation sent straight from hell. They came in demonic packs. Evil forest giants, the head demons that were servants of the Halfling, their watchers and dwellers of hell that they once met, the twins guided the group in both worlds by night and deliberated in the purgatory world, and their underground demonic vampire followers attacked the innocent souls. The Halflings. They were just like Satan but more skilled. They were actually relatives from each others through Lucifer and Medusa, except with greater powers since the twins took over Satan's charge in dooming hell created from severe worlds with the knowledge gained by their trip traveling and discovering severe villages in the purgatory world that Satan couldn't put his feet into. They mislead some of the innocent spirits to the airport. They had fun with their crime without noticing they were actually in the pursuit of becoming long lasting demons in human and wolf form. Until the 13th of the day they hauled upon innocent souls and turned it into an entity that gives light and can't be seen with bare eye by humans except by divines, beasts, creatures and shrubberies from hell and the purgatory world, dumped them into the waters, that would slowly shrunk by the color blue or red that the lost soul sheens. The color strongly depended on the command of for the deaths of earthly innocent souls or purgatory innocent shrubberies, creatures or beasts. The place where it happens on planet earth turns into a crime with police surroundings and forensic services. The radio would speak of an inhumanly disaster that couldn't be solved. A case that couldn't be completed.

Both twins became commanders, of the pack, most shrubberies, creatures and beasts couldn't believe their destiny, they didn't want it, but it happened, and it was already to late. Both Halflings turned into evils and demons of hell, into one of the most malevolent mighty demons above Satan. Into criminals with a criminal mind. Uriela was no longer a virgin and had sex with everyone with her brothers desire that she kissed while making love to other beasts. She on top of beasts in the witness of his brother and he also wanted to join the sex game. They were supposed to travel after the sex game adventure. Where they would go, they had no clue. They were clueless. Before leaving the sea, they committed multiple crimes on homes on people they didn't care about. They sucked the spirit out of the people living in those homes and committed multiple attacks to feed the hunger of their demonic workforce. They sucked the souls out of the people who lived there

and they made sure they ran darn
hard away. As soon as they had
what they wanted, just before as
they had what they wanted, they
heard the sirens and the cops came.
The Halflings slept during daylight,
and awakened at night. It was
midnight again. They became
malevolent but they felt wicked.
Both went back to hell and gave the
friendly giant diamonds and gold,
rocks. The Halflings gave the
creatures and beasts that raised
them items. Each item resembled
something from their birth from
their parents that bonded them with
powers above hell. They whispered
in their thoughts that they had to
burn it in their cages they were kept
in as slaves. Burn it once situations
would get even worse in Superbia
that was already darkened. The
beasts, creatures and shrubberies
cried and wondered why? They

sensed something affecting the Halflings. The Halflings told them that this was the best option to get rid of all the demons on planet earth and in the purgatory world. Something that their parents longed for a long time ago. The Halflings told their family, the beasts, creatures and shrubberies of Superbia that they would never return and they said goodbye to their birds, trees and animals, relatives and family.

The fires in Dorthrin started to redeem while both twins were slowly losing their powers. After their ancestors couldn't get hold of the reversing spell from the deepest fires from hell to keep the Halflings in hell for eternal, the items that the Halflings gave to their raisers, Satan decided to take the Halflings as fast as possible into the yacht while slowly losing their powers and

Satan, he became mad. The Halflings didn't care, because they didn't want to have this malevolent curse in the first place. Especially because they chose it out of love. The Halflings decided to jump off the boat into the water to decrease their pain. But Satan and his assistance did it too. The pain didn't go away. Because of the Sea's water they regained their power by noshing themselves with the entities of blameless and remorseful souls and the Halflings stayed a victim in crime.

At night the Halflings experimented with their devilish powers as well as their spells once heard by showing the qualities they were looking for in their next life on earth once the love is over between them and their demonic ghostly friends, being realistic. The Halflings pulled the contract that was now a paper in flames and sprayed it with their own blood that they kept in a thin bottle, they fold it into an envelope and put it into a jar. The Halflings held glooming Dandelions in their hands, while picturing their skeleton lovers of darkness and they would throw away the jar into the sea's water and picture themselves with the ghost friends for eternity. The Halflings blew the glooming Dandelions into the air of politeness and the remaining leaves into the envelope and sealed it with a kiss of their blood. With blood on their lips from the evil curse that was all a set up the moment the demonic friendly ghosts were sent to bring the twins back to hell. A secret once revealed.

"yes" did not always mean "yes" among both friends. In order to avoid conflict with demons and maintain smooth in, pleasant relations, both rarely said "no" directly. "Yes" may have meant "maybe" or "I'll consider it." "A negative reply was unlikely to be fulfilled, the "yes" both told demons was actually a "no", but was probably misunderstood by demons.

The twins, both smiled to transfer kindness and goodwill. But then demonic friends who took them away in their flight of growth nearby the Sea saw it as a gate to take the Halflings into crime. The expressions of the Halflings were maybe too smooth, but in their sight awkward or embarrassing if they wouldn't smile that may appear inappropriate. The distance between the Halflings and the beasts, shrubberies, creatures of Superbia became a greater distance when talking about imprint language. The Halflings would never see them after the spell. The spell could only be undone if the demonic ghost friends relationship would have received the jar with the bleeding kiss stamped with the Dandelions leaves. Or only if, their parents would receive the jar to burn it.

The Halflings started to feel their heart beat. The Halflings looked at their ghostly friends in crime with a sparkling imprint of their parents and held both their hands close to their hearts. They lost their powers in darkness alongside their fading ghostly wannabe friends into the gates of hell. Their final call upon the opening gates "It is good to have you my twin, my other wholly part of my heart, hold my hand, we will walk through this life together. Twin, my other half, it is good to have you, my soul, my heart, my protector, my shiny star for life." Satan became more foolish and furious. The Halflings said: "Guys, it is too late." They went to hell and back. It was like a journey through a traveling machine into space to survive from a coma. They thought they would never wake up and knew what was behind those gates of Satan's glory. It wasn't shining at all. The demons voices where tempting behind the gates of hell and said "yes" in slithering tone, "yes you!" It wasn't their time yet. They where swallowed in a passageway and moved back on the beaches of the Sea.

The flames in their eyes turned from red flames to none, the flaming stopped when their hearts was released from their ghostly friends. The Halflings showed, their pure loving hearts and beyond. The black and white shadows of their souls, between their morning water sports and their afternoon music symphony. They concentrated on the scent of their lost hearts from the blood and fire that made them waft off their love promise while Satan was speaking of his return in madness. A sign had gripped them tight and only their senses that squeezed between their lungs could take in what was left of them. Hell is loveless and soulless. The Halflings could smell the liquid death of sinners.

The creatures, shrubberies and beasts from Superbia had received the jar and burnt it with a poison that cured the Halflings. They had the power to kill those who inflicted their malevolent change. They got set free. Unchained by the friendly giant.

The Halflings took a deep breath and let it out. Both recognize flowers, birds, and trees. Both stand in front of the glass door with a golden handle with a stained glass pattern in the window. Then Uriela pushes the golden door handle down and lets herself into the hall. The hotel is even more beautiful than she had imagined in her mind in her mother's letters. Everything is dazzling with the statue of Maria in the corner of the rooms.

International flight. Both wonder about their mother, her standing in a business suit. Both imprint their mother and father with the question why their parents saw everyone as a sexual being, if not. A bliss that brought satisfaction into their everyday life. As both twins grew older their flirting soon became a small touch, a secret smile, looking at each other just a little too long.

The Halflings understood how their mother chose her victims by the same curiosity and sin in life, naughty touches and look in the eyes.

"Almost all ours" both Halflings said with a wink.

It was a naughty look from the 1001 nights of Arabia.

Together they wander through the hotel.

The Halflings came in with their sunglasses and a cap, which made guests gaze. It was as wonderful as in who-gives-a-fuck attitude. Both had the guests captivated with their cheerfulness by the piano in the hallway and a guitar. Some creatures, shrubberies and beasts could recognize them from a far that they were familiar divines. Mischievous eyes – check, curiosity – check, insecure – check, clumsy – check. They ought to be bloodline of two worlds with resembles of their mother L. The Halflings didn't only talk about themselves, their talent to conquer the world! Both were young still and their energy was perfect.

At night they were guided to the hotel kitchen. It was no secret, they were invited by a wolf in human form to prepare an elite feast. She was wearing a Bordeaux dress. Equal to mother's lips. He was wearing a three-piece-suite. They looked damned hot.

They were in an occupied hotel. Their mother's hotel. La Royal Smile Hotel.

It was a paradise. It was quiet, heavenly, and perfect. Everything was in bloom. They took another deep breath.

Once grown, both Halflings had a soft spot in their hearts for their parents, they didn't know exactly why. Both got caught gazing into the galaxy and kissed one another softly as siblings. Both had been reserved, but both couldn't feel the longing of each other's bodies.

Both longed to be closer to their parents.

A champagne bottle popped open in the hotel and 2 glasses of champagne were filled. "And so a new adventure begins. All ours now"

"Just the way we wanted"

The Halflings became "Fed at last, free at last"

No love, no matter how many years spent rotting, can tell the future. The accidental flight took the balance of the Halflings' life away. It's a reminder, that an unconditional love can make you wander around in danger causing evil roads that eventually can break realizing that life was happily in little things and joyfulness living with the imprints from parents, loved ones that seem smaller than they are. Love on earth or in the purgatory world is not related to love felt in a soulless hell.

The stars and moon are getting close.

The lost souls in the sea cry.

The twins knew how to conjure the appalling versatility of their criminal possibility into a peacock's tail of their own oeuvre.

The Halflings live happily together for eternity in Droplet Cloud. The demonic ghostly friends went to hell and faded away in the sea and new demonic entities lights at last join in the sea.

Heartbreaks were brutal. They could smell blood from a distance. Blood was related to life. Their parent's shade of death was perceptible in dreams and flames. Raphael and Uriela their bond could never be broken. By a cut both could feed each other and have a taste of blood from an open wound that bonded their souls for eternity in hell. Following the flames the crows left, no matter what the price tag. The twins fashioned dreams of their parents in every moment. Nobody knew that this was it. The end of their adventure. Where their darkened souls destroyed life after considering the great adventure, letting the familiar and the unfamiliar define who they truest were. Their heart wanted to be loved unconditionally only with no secrets. They secretly knew about the covenant with hell.

They created a great power in their wondering from their parents' unconditional love and uniqueness. Not their love or death drew the limit, but a fading memory, a disappearance of enlightened friends and another letter read, from the thought of their life. As children they weren't in need of high care. Blooming flowers, trees, beasts and animals raised them. And so the adventure began. A beastly adventure. A new cause, a new adventure, a new passion in love without secrets. They stayed together with all their temper, whether they were foolish or not. Whether their hearts was sometimes to busy and couldn't overlook their destiny anymore. They were just themselves staying with each other in the moment while they lived. They'll never need anything else than the love that will always remain for each other and the way they are right now. In the offing until the next disaster. It was a perfect adventure to end and cheers upon.

Part 26

"Atomic bombs", "l'arme de gaz". It appeared once more in severe technology systems about the pledges that the twins committed, but seldom sparingly. The twins preferred "flow like water". There was uncertainty about the conflict they created among innocent humans. There was need of time to look at the disaster they created in the darkness of hell and the civilized world. It was war that could easily be solved. They became the snoopers and thought they were the only one that had the power of a water flow, but they could also trigger the "energy weapon" that their parents once launched. Is there actually a flow like water? It was a wind farm to grab the power to save themselves from the rival, Satan. It was a enchanting story. This because of the twins pledging sins to kill innocent humans. The let go and free the pain of losing their father and mother. It thought them to question about the life they were living. Just like Satan and other more than human.

Their growth. They had hope and a motherfucking middle finger to hell. The transition from darkness to light was also a study of nature. They brushed their teeth, took demonic meals and in-between gigantic fruit, vegetables and magical milk from hell and Dorthrin. They had swimming classes, did water sports, were rested in the mornings after committing sinful crimes beyond. They were just confronted with unknown places without the guidance of their parents, that within moments changed into hell's desires and to out rule Satan. Uriela and Raphael were crueler than once before. They had the ability to fly.

Satan was surprised. He was totally surprised. The twins were in that time unique and were not fooled by Satanist idiots. They became malevolent hero's who fought for the love of their father and mother. The death attack on innocent humans was all over the world in Dorthrin. According to the letters of their parents they assumed their parents committed suicide after a murder to people the twins hunted upon. Rumors say that the kill of their father's faith was upon an innocent man who raped their mother and that of children. The last masterpiece of pedophiles who fuck younger children confirmed the twins their principles of innocent soul to soul destruction in a planned way as they undertook the strike on their mother's destiny. Before the dawn, the twins found out that there were executions placed and planned on their families in Dorthrin by dwellers. Every crime inflicted by the twins made the system go crazy. Phoenixes and wolf pets. Beautiful creatures that were destroyed in their world at time of ruling over Satan's grounds. They were going to the end of times.

The letters Uriela and Raphael sent to their parents was about many stuff. L and S traveled through a heavenly time machine to see their twins. They traveled back to time with an airplane. The last plane had an accident and crashed. Once the twins arrived at home they burned every living immortal in hell and returned to heavenly earth. "Now that we're back, I want to have a hug, I'm spent, all tuckered out and dowsy." A full sisterly desire. They were poised to fight, afraid of heights it would ruin over their love secrets, a keen riding over truth.

L and S thought by watching their children growing it would be the rising from everything. They lived together old and heavenly. With faltering steps out of the gate of heaven, then back again. The twins walked through the halls of the hotel and saw a phenomenon above the statue of Maria. The twins and more and more beasts, creatures and animals were beginning to see them straight on glimmering and for a period of time. It was an active imprint and a dream come true. Their spirit was misty and white, vaporous in a heavenly form appearance, shadows of their parents. Their children and parents imprints bonded in an enchanting way perfected beyond ordinary sights, the gate that lead to spaces of higher consciousness with deeply enchanting abilities to feel their love and envision heavenly souls.

The twins realized that their parents were some kind of smokers. It was good stuff. Hell yeah. It seemed like the Sensation white instead of the finals. The twins promised to write letters. Putting the letters they wrote with their own handwriting in bottles so it could travel safely through a water flow. Bottle mail from a different universe, with their secretly Wolverhampton crying Latin. The nice thing about those letters is that they make much larger impression than worries. But what the hack. We all know this kind of parental story. Shelter. Glimmering twins. With their hearts passionately full. Such as this can't be forgotten. Their mothers precious smile and their fathers clumsiness. They spent a whole night drinking and smoking, talking about all sorts of stuff that their parents missed telling them. The glasses of wine kept on

pouring and the children loved it.
The twins talked about their
adventures in both worlds. It was
precious glimmering time. The twins
asked for a kiss. They received a kiss
on their forehead. Amazed by their
parents kiss. It all seemed
miraculous. A magical reunion that
only existed in their dreams and
history. They prepared themselves
on the best.

Acknowledgement

I have so many wonderful and lovingly
people to thank as a guilty pleasure
with love for helping this book reach
the public. At first I want to thank *Ja*
and *Ma* and my publisher, thank you
for your passionate cooperation after
reading "Beyond Unconditional Love".
They have shown their expression full
enthusiasm from the clouds and
support to continue my writings.

I wishfully thank *Fe* and *Lu* because
together we stood on top of the clouds.
And when *San* and *Ty* joined with us
something magical came to existence in
the creation. Also thanks to *Family Oat.*
that did so much to make this book
reach a new audience and to notice it to
the public.

Also special thanks to the entire
promotion team that I'm tremendously
thankfully for promoting my writings.

Everybody has worked so hard and has put their very best and showed much enthusiasm in the creation.

I also want to thank the many readers and critics of "Beyond Unconditional Love" and this book "Unconditional Secrets Beyond Love" who read the book first and than recommended the rest of the world to read the book. They still do this, for this book, with many thanks.

I also wishfully thank the *Angels and Wizards* for their love, support and input to make this book famous to the rest of the world. Thou are true wizards and angels to me!

Biography

Marlies van den Broek, M.B van den Broek (born in Kenya; December 1986) is a Sagittarius and was a former ballerina who rose to worldwide fame as a writer. She practiced dancing at the age of 5 until the age of 22 years in many dancing disciplines and won competition prizes on top 3 rankings of every given contest. She grew up nearby Stone Town in Zanzibar and was raised spending most of her time in Rock City and Dar es Salaam. Her after school activities was going to ballet and during holidays she would travel through the Serengeti. Once her parents decided to make the big move to Europe, she continued dancing in more disciplines than ballet and swimming only. Her parents loved to travel. This added to the development of her to travel as well to countries within Europe. She was very sporty and practiced severe water sports rather than winter sports. She graduated from University and had a successful career within an American company in the Aerospace and Military industry situated in Miami. Her last ballet performance was in 2012 and this was the last dance saved with the time to quit, to change and focus on a different discipline. She has lived a part of her life in Paris. In Paris is where it all started and she received a contract to release her writings. She is an author of her favorites consisting of poetry "Love, Life, Future and Happiness" and romance fiction book "Beyond Unconditional Love", the most successful and critical book of popular books in the top 10 of best romance fiction. She has followers all around the world with focus in the USA and Canada. Overall the public wanted more of her sold work of "Beyond Unconditional Love". This is the reason she has been working on a new book as a follow up "Unconditional Secrets Beyond Love". It is a wonder that Marlies could still write, this is precisely the egg from which the white swam emerged. Talent is of course in explicable. One either has it or one doesn't. but whoever wants to do something with it finds himself, to his surprise, more supported by his virtues than by his bad qualities. With her ideas she was also far ahead of her time. Concentration and the scientific humility to climb the highest mountain of her ladders time and time again. This enabled her to start writing a following to her earlier book "Beyond Unconditional Love", which has been preserved from her to start with: the adventures of the children of L and S, and she created imperishable figures. Where she had broken her leg everywhere, the exaggeration. She could finally be herself. Without any concession to credibility, she put a new book in the world that is entirely hers. She is a madly gifted person in society. The question of who wrote this book "Unconditional Secrets Beyond Love" has been solved. But even here some complications arise. "I got a pair of new pumps which I used to decorate the

cover of my first and second book,
although worn a few times."